KNOCKOUT!

Hardin took a step and Slocum turned, just in time to duck Hardin's sucker punch. Moving in tight, Slocum nailed him with a combination, a left hooking into Hardin's gut and a right cross cracking into the jaw. Hardin staggered back and sat down hard.

"Nice punch," Matt said, laughing. "I expect you may have boxed your way out of a job."

"That he has," Stuart snapped. "I won't stand for that sort of thing in my home. Get your gear and get off my land, Slocum—now!"

OTHER BOOKS BY JAKE LOGAN

RIDE, SLOCUM, RIDE
SIXGUN CEMETERY
SLOCUM'S DEADLY GAME
HIGH, WIDE, AND DEADLY
SLOCUM AND THE WILD STALLION CHASE
SLOCUM AND THE LAREDO SHOWDOWN
SLOCUM AND THE CLAIM JUMPERS
SLOCUM AND THE CHEROKEE MANHUNT
SIXGUNS AT SILVERADO
SLOCUM AND THE EL PASO BLOOD FEUD
SLOCUM AND THE BLOOD RAGE
SLOCUM AND THE CRACKER CREEK KILLERS
GUNFIGHTER'S GREED
SIXGUN LAW
SLOCUM AND THE ARIZONA KIDNAPPERS
SLOCUM AND THE HANGING TREE
SLOCUM AND THE ABILENE SWINDLE
BLOOD AT THE CROSSING
SLOCUM AND THE BUFFALO HUNTERS
SLOCUM AND THE PREACHER'S DAUGHTER
SLOCUM AND THE GUNFIGHTER'S RETURN
THE RAWHIDE BREED
GOLD FEVER
DEATH TRAP
SLOCUM AND THE CROOKED JUDGE
SLOCUM AND THE TONG WARRIORS
SLOCUM AND THE OUTLAW'S TRAIL
SLOW DEATH
SLOCUM AND THE PLAINS MASSACRE
SLOCUM AND THE IDAHO BREAKOUT
STALKER'S MOON
MEXICAN SILVER
SLOCUM'S DEBT
SLOCUM AND THE CATTLE WAR
COLORADO KILLERS
RIDE TO VENGEANCE
REVENGE OF THE GUNFIGHTER
TEXAS TRAIL DRIVE

JAKE LOGAN
THE WYOMING CATTLE WAR

B
BERKLEY BOOKS, NEW YORK

THE WYOMING CATTLE WAR

A Berkley Book/published by arrangement with
the author

PRINTING HISTORY
Berkley edition/June 1990

All rights reserved.
Copyright © 1990 by The Berkley Publishing Group.
This book may not be reproduced in whole or in part, by
mimeograph or any other means, without permission.
For information address: The Berkley Publishing Group,
200 Madison Avenue, New York, New York 10016.

ISBN: 0-425-12137-2

A BERKLEY BOOK® TM 757,375
Berkley Books are published by The Berkley Publishing Group,
200 Madison Avenue, New York, New York 10016.
The name "BERKLEY" and the "B" logo
are trademarks belonging to Berkley Publishing Corporation.

PRINTED IN THE UNITED STATES OF AMERICA

10 9 8 7 6 5 4 3 2 1

THE WYOMING CATTLE WAR

1

The sky overhead looked as if it stretched forever. John Slocum reined in his horse and took his hat in one hand while he jerked a bright bandanna from his pocket and mopped his brow. The slippery film of sweat and dust came away like paste. He knew without thinking about it that he looked like some new brave, taking a first stab at war paint. The bandanna bore smears of mud and he shook it, but the sticky dirt clung to the cloth.

He'd never been afraid of work. Part of him even felt guilty when he was out of a job. But this Wyoming cow country was something new, enough to make a grown man cry. As big as Texas was, it was at least familiar. The work, the other hands, even the weather, all were things he'd known by genus if not by species. But Wyoming was different. As different as the Sioux were from the Comanche.

Sure, he still wore his butt raw sitting in a saddle for twelve- and fourteen-hour days. He still had to wrestle calves to the ground, still had the stink of burnt hair and charred skin in his nostrils. Hell, he thought, he even had the same damn blisters on his hands. What with the rope and the branding iron, it seemed like his fingers would never straighten out enough to deal a hand of poker. All that was familiar.

But Wyoming was just not Texas, or Kansas. And Addison Arthur Stuart, the III yet, was just not like any man he'd ever worked for before. Stuart owned cows, just as many head as Chisum or Goodnight. But he didn't talk like either man, and he sure as hell didn't think like either one.

Taking a pull of tepid water from his canteen, he wondered why he'd ever been curious about England. If Stuart was typical, and he'd bet a month's pay on it, Slocum had lost his taste for foreign travel. The man didn't know the rules, and was hell bent to make up a set of his own. The worst of it was that Stuart ignored the best advice he was getting, advice from men like Larry Holt, who'd been a trail boss for more than a half-dozen trips up from the Panhandle into Kansas. Ignoring a man like Holt, who knew what was what and how things were supposed to be done, was courting disaster.

And that snooty accent didn't help matters. Stuart sounded like a fool even when he was right. Between the accent and the way he carried himself, like everybody ought to believe him because he had a roman numeral after his name, and a three parter at that, Stuart had managed to make himself the laughingstock of half the open range among the hired hands. His comrades in the Stock Growers' Association seemed more tolerant. Of course, some of them had the same accent.

Slocum heard the hooves, but couldn't see clearly into the bright sun. Mopping his brow once more, he shielded his eyes with the hat without putting it on. Just visible behind a cloud of swirling dust, about a hundred head of cattle came pounding down a long, gentle slope. Three men, yipping and waving their hats, were hard on their tails. Slocum groaned inwardly, knowing the cattle were cows with their calves. Another fifty head, ready for branding.

Clapping his hat back on his head, Slocum tucked the bandanna away, then kicked his mount out toward the charging herd. As the newcomers drew closer, he could make out their faces through the dust. Clay Hardin, the one man he didn't like on the Stuart spread, was riding point now, the cattle bellowing and starting to slow down.

Slocum dismounted at the big bonfire and stuck the four branding irons back in, resting the brands on a log in the heart of the crackling flames. Hardin rode over and doffed his hat, clapping dust from his chaps and rubbing a grubby shirtsleeve across his brow.

"You get them other beeves marked, Slocum?"

"All done."

"Got some more for you, fifty, maybe sixty." Hardin glanced behind him, into the western mountains. "Like to get them done before sundown."

"We can manage."

"Where's Russ?"

"Something spooked a dozen head. They ran off, but we were able to keep the rest of the beeves calm. Should be back soon as he runs them down."

"Who's earmarking?"

"Russ was."

"I guess you are, then, 'til Russ gets back."

"It's tough enough roping and branding. You keep running them in here faster than the two of us could finish 'em. I don't know about getting them all done by myself."

"You better try, Slocum. Lots of men out there lookin' for work. You don't want to, maybe we can find somebody who does."

"You saying I'm not working, Hardin?"

"Nope! You are. And Mr. Stuart don't take kindly to people who accept his money and don't give him nothing in exchange."

"Then get out of here and let me get to work."

"That's more like it, Slocum. That's a lot more like it."

Slocum ignored him and snatched a short lariat from his saddle. Draping the rope over his shoulder, he tugged on a pair of leather gloves, wincing as the rough hide scraped over his blisters.

Hardin laughed. "Wyoming'll make a man out of you, you don't look out, Slocum."

The other two cowboys had walked their horses over and sat listening, their hands draped over their saddle horns. Both of them looked dead tired, but they were following the exchange intently. Slocum wondered how a man like Larry Holt, who was about as decent and professional a boss as he'd ever had, could put up with the likes of Hardin. He asked more than one of the other hands, but when the subject was Clay Hardin, nobody seemed to have anything to say.

Holt himself had declined to answer when Slocum had put the question directly to him. But Larry had more to worry about than what one cowhand thought of another or, for that matter, what all of them thought of one man. Even if that man was his second in command.

Slocum mounted the chopping horse and nudged it into a walk without saying anything to Hardin. He could feel the other man's eyes on his back. He could feel, too, the electric expectation crackling in the air. The other hands seemed to be waiting for some sort of explosion. But Slocum needed the work. He couldn't take the risk that Hardin had as much clout as he pretended with Addison Stuart.

He circled the knot of new cattle, taking a rough count of the unbranded yearlings. At the same time, he did a rough tally of the cows. Half a dozen, maybe more, looked like they didn't even belong to Stuart at all. Stuart stock had the distinctive swallowtail notch on the tip of the ear, and quite a few of the newly rounded-up stock didn't have it. And if the mothers didn't have it, they weren't Stuart's and neither were the calves.

Working his way carefully through the nervous steers, he got a rope on one that looked like it didn't belong. He tugged it through the outer fringe of the small herd, then dropped down for a closer look, pulling himself toward the skittish cow along the taut lariat.

Even before he reached it, he realized he was right. The cow's ear had been notched just above the head, a double V cut into the loose flesh. The cow's yearling circled around its mother, as if it were trying to figure out what would happen next.

"Hey, Slocum, what the hell are you doing?"

Slocum turned as Hardin pushed his horse into a canter, the horse turning almost broadside under the sharp prodding of Hardin's spurs.

"This one isn't ours," Slocum said, loosening the rope and tossing the loop free of the cow's head.

"*Ours*, did you say?"

"That's what I said."

"Since when is Stuart stock any of yours. You a relative, or did Mr. Stuart just sell you a piece of the ranch when I wasn't looking?"

"You know what I mean, Hardin. This cow doesn't belong to Mr. Stuart."

"You a lawyer, too, besides being a cowboy? Come to think of it, you do kinda work stock like you never done it before. Maybe you ain't a cowhand at all. Maybe you're *just* a lawyer. That it?"

"Nope."

"Then what the hell are you wasting time for? Brand that little sucker and..." He jumped from the saddle, letting the reins trail behind him. Fists clenched, he stormed over to Slocum.

"Can't do that, Clay."

"Why not?"

"It's illegal. You ought to know that. Hell, Mr. Stuart is a big wheel in the Stock Growers' Association. I don't think he'd take too kindly to it, either."

"Slocum, you better..."

He stopped and cocked an ear. Slocum heard it too,

a distant crack, like the snapping of a huge, dry stick. It echoed across the rolling buffalo grass.

"What the hell was that?"

"Sounded like a gunshot to me," one of the other hands said. Slocum glanced at him, to see if he was joking. The cowboy, a tall, rail-thin man known only as Scarecrow, or the shorter Crow, was standing in his stirrups. "Over that way," he said, pointing with one impossibly long arm.

Slocum coiled his rope and mounted up.

"Where the hell you think you're going, Slocum?"

"That's where Russ went. If that was a gunshot, he might need some help."

Before Hardin could argue, three more cracks, this time clearly gunshots, echoed over the ridge, then came back, much diminished, from another, higher ridge behind them.

Slocum didn't wait for permission. He kicked the horse and it spurted forward. Like most chopping horses, it could turn on a dime and go from a standing start to full speed with little more than a gentle flex of the knees. Some cowhands swore that a good chopping horse didn't even need a rider to do its ordinary job, cutting stock from a larger herd.

Slocum glanced back to see if anyone was going to follow him. Hardin was already in the saddle, and the two hands with him wheeled their horses to fall in behind. Another shot echoed over the grassland, and Slocum prodded his horse to go still faster. Behind him, he could hear the hooves of the three horses. Near the top of the rise, he reined back a little. Not knowing what lay on the far side, he decided to play it safe.

Hardin and the others caught him as he broke over the ridge and started down the other side. Hardin shouted something, but Slocum didn't catch what it was. In the still-bright sun, it was hard to see far without squinting. The glare was almost thick, like some sort of yellow jelly smeared over his eyes.

Far below, on the valley floor, a small cluster of cows

milled in a circle, bellowing with fear. Another shot cracked across the valley, bouncing back twice, then dying away. The cattle bolted, thundering back up the slope toward him, and Slocum was forced to swing around them. A stand of cottonwoods stood almost dead center right behind where the cattle had been, and that seemed to be the source of the last shot.

Slocum bore down on it as someone bolted from the far side.

"Russ?" Slocum shouted. "Russ, you alright?"

No one answered and Slocum dismounted while his horse was still moving. He jerked a Winchester from his boot and sprinted into the trees, where he could just make out the big sorrel Russ had been riding. The other rider was hightailing it across the valley, and Slocum could see a checkered shirt and white hat on the rider, but not his face. The horse, a nondescript chestnut, was running flat out as Slocum shouted again.

Pushing the underbrush aside with the barrel of the Winchester, he nearly stumbled over Russ, lying on his side, curled into a ball. Slocum dropped to one knee as Hardin and the others broke into the clear, having rounded the cottonwoods and splashed through the shallow creek on the valley floor.

He reached down and took Russ by the shoulder, shaking him gently, but the cowhand didn't move. He groaned once, almost a whisper, and Slocum pushed him onto his back. Russ unfurled like a flag in the wind, his arms flopping on the grass and lying still.

The bloodstained shirt hid what had to be a bad wound. Slocum bent close as Russ tried to speak. His lips moved, but no sound came out, then the lips stopped moving. The eyes, full of pain, were extraordinarily bright for a moment, then they seemed to go out, like candles.

Slocum didn't need another look to know that Russ Higgins was dead.

2

There was nothing he could do for Russ Higgins. Slocum reached out with a thumb and closed the blue eyes, already beginning to glaze over. They looked surprised, as if something had caught him when he least expected it. Slocum had seen enough men die to know it was always a surprise. And he expected his own eyes would have that same wide-open stare, as if they were trying to see right through the bottom of the sky, when his time came, as it surely would.

He vaulted into the saddle, not bothering to boot the Winchester. Something told him he was going to have use for it sooner than he'd like. Hardin and the others were already little more than spots drifting through the grass. So far away, they seemed barely to be moving. The chopping horse took off after them, and Slocum wondered who in the hell would have had reason to shoot Higgins. The man minded his own business. All he'd tried to do was run down a few head of spooked cattle and push them back for branding. That was no killing offense anywhere, even if the cattle belonged to someone else. Hell, Russ hadn't even had the chance to check them out.

And if that *was* the reason, Slocum realized only too well it could have been him instead of Russ lying there with the five-mile stare. He started to close on Hardin, who was still whipping his mount every few strides, lashing alternate sides with the reins and digging his spurs into the animal's hide. They were less than a quarter mile ahead of him when all three started shooting.

Slocum kicked his horse again, goosing it into a full gallop. The animal seemed to fly over the top of the thick buffalo grass, its hooves barely making contact with the thick sod beneath. It would have been exhilarating, not unlike the races he remembered from Georgia days. But it wasn't fun, not with a dead man lying on his back at the starting line.

Slocum closed to within fifty yards as Hardin plunged over the ridge and on into the next valley. As near as Slocum could tell, no one was returning fire. As he rose up over the ridge line, he could see their quarry far in the distance. Out of range even of a big Sharps buffalo gun, the rider was killing his mount to open up an even bigger lead. If they eased up and laid on his trail, they wouldn't have to catch him. The tired horse would come back to them in short order. But Hardin kept pushing, as if he were determined, for some reason Slocum couldn't figure, to get there first.

Hardin was out front, and he emptied his revolver a second time as Slocum caught up with them.

"Why don't you ease up, Clay? He can't keep this up," Slocum shouted.

"Mind your own damn business, Reb."

Scarecrow looked at Slocum and shook his head, as if to say, why waste your breath? Slocum was about to shout back when Hardin's horse stumbled. The stallion went down hard, and Hardin flew forward, tumbling over the horse's neck. The horse shook its mane and tried repeatedly to get up. One foreleg clearly had been broken. Scarecrow reined in and urged his mount back before jumping down and running to the horse. He rushed right past Hardin to get to the injured stallion.

Slocum, too, wheeled his horse and leapt from the saddle. He knelt beside the unconscious Hardin and felt for a pulse. He found a faint throb in Hardin's neck and loosened the foreman's neckerchief. Hardin's eyes were closed, and a thin trickle of blood seeped from one corner of his mouth, running down his chin and dripping on his shirt.

The remaining hand continued on a few hundred yards and fired three or four futile shots before reining in. He turned his own mount and trotted back in a rather leisurely manner. Slocum tried to make Hardin comfortable. He winced when he heard the gunshot and turned to see Scarecrow holstering his big Colt revolver.

Joining Slocum, but not bothering to kneel, he said, "Too bad it couldn't've been the other way around."

Slocum glanced up, the question evident in his puzzled frown.

"Shoot the man and save the horse," Scarecrow explained. "Sometimes I think there ain't no justice."

Slocum didn't answer, but the third hand cackled. "That's a good one, Crow. I reckon that'll make the rounds of the bunkhouse tonight."

"Not if you know what's good for you, Carson."

"Good for you, you mean," Carson corrected.

"Crow, get this wet in the creek over there, will you?" Slocum held the bandanna up and Scarecrow snatched at it with some distaste. "Rather tighten the damn thing around his neck."

"Grab an end, Crow, and I'll get the other one," Carson snickered.

Slocum ignored them both. When Scarecrow saw he couldn't get a rise out of Slocum, he walked off through the brush. He wasn't exactly rushing, but at least he was moving, Slocum thought.

THE WYOMING CATTLE WAR 11

Carson stayed on his horse, his palms stacked on his pommel. "You'll learn, Slocum."

Slocum looked up. "Learn what?"

"You'll see. It always takes the new hands a while. It's like anything else, I guess—learning to ride, learning to shoot. Hell, learning how to drink and cuss, even. You got to work at it."

"And exactly what is it I am working at?"

"Reading Clay Hardin. You think he'll be grateful, don't you?"

"I expect so, although that's not why I'm trying to help him. He's hurt. Hell, if I were hurt, I'd want help."

"Sure you would. Me too. Only thing is, that was you or me lyin' there, Hardin wouldn't lift a finger. He'd probably dock you a day's pay for loafing. That's just the kind of man he is. I reckon he can't help it, but that don't make it right. And he's always doing stuff like that, sucking up to that asshole we work for."

"You dislike it so much, why do you stay?"

"I got to eat, Slocum. See, things are kind of sewed up around here. You know what I mean?"

"No. Why don't you tell me."

"Maybe later."

Slocum heard rustling in the underbrush and wondered why Carson wouldn't want to talk in front of Scarecrow. Before he could figure it out, the tall man, looking more like a praying mantis than a human being, stilted out of the brush and tossed a soaking bandanna Slocum's way.

"Here you go, cowboy. See maybe you can drown the bastard with that. Cool him off some, anyways."

Slocum draped the water-cooled cloth over Hardin's forehead and propped him up a little.

"You see who did the shooting?" Slocum asked.

"Naw. Didn't get half close enough," Carson said. "Whoever he was, he sure must have had it in for old Russ, though. Plugged him deader'n a doornail, didn't he?"

"No idea who would want to kill him?"

"No, sir, none. I don't believe it was personal, though. Almost surely not."

"Why do you say that?"

"You're a new hand, Slocum. There's stuff going on around here you don't know nothing about. You're probably better off you don't learn anything about them, neither."

"If it could get me killed, maybe I *ought* to know about it."

"Man's got a point, son," Scarecrow said.

"You tell 'im, then," Carson responded. "Me, I believe I'll keep my mouth shut."

"How about one of you men going back to the remuda and picking up a spare mount for Hardin?" Slocum asked.

"I'll go," Carson said. "I'm already up." Without another word, he kicked his horse into motion, prodding it into a fast walk with his spurs. Slocum watched him go, then turned to Scarecrow. "Crow, maybe you can get his gear ready. Strip the saddle. I don't think any bones are broken, so we can get him up on a horse when he comes to."

Almost as if he'd heard, Hardin moaned. Slocum watched the eyes flutter, then stay open. They had a vacant look, as if Hardin were confronted by strangers.

"You alright, Hardin?" Slocum asked.

Hardin groaned again and tried to sit up. Slocum pressed him back with the flat of one hand, and Hardin didn't struggle.

"You alright?" Slocum asked again.

"What happened?" Hardin asked.

"You took a pretty bad spill."

Hardin tried again to sit up. This time, he struggled against the pressure of Slocum's hand. He looked around for his horse, spotted the stallion, the ugly black hole in the center of its skull, and shook his head. "Damn..."

"Anything hurt?"

"My whole damn body hurts. What the hell is going on?"

"Somebody killed Russ Higgins. You and Crow and Carson were chasing him when your horse stepped in a hole. He broke his leg and Crow put him away."

"It's starting to come back to me now. A little, anyhow."

"Sonny's gone to get you a horse. Think you can ride or should we bring a buckboard?"

"I'll be alright, I think. Help me up." He snatched at the wet cloth still clinging to his forehead and tucked it into his shirt pocket.

Slocum stood, then reached down for Hardin's outstretched hand. When he was back on his feet, he snatched his hand away and took a couple of steps. He started to fall, and Slocum reached out to steady him.

"Maybe you ought to sit down until Carson gets back."

"Maybe you should mind your own business, Slocum. I'm alright. Just leave me be."

"Have it your way."

"Oh, I will. You can bank on it."

"Hard nose, aren't you?" Slocum asked, trying to joke him into a better mood.

"The hardest you ever seen, I'll tell you that."

"Maybe you should bend a little, so you don't break," Slocum said.

"Don't worry about me breaking."

"Whatever you say."

Slocum gave up. If Hardin wanted to pretend he was invincible, let him. A man gets a hair up his ass, you might as well stand back and let him go. You usually can't stop him, and most times, if you can, the chances are he won't thank you for your trouble.

"You get a look at the bushwhacker?" Slocum asked.

"Never mind what I saw. Last I heard, Russ worked for Mr. Stuart. I'll tell him what I saw, not you."

"Stuart ain't going to like it, no matter what you saw," Scarecrow suggested.

"That's his problem, and mine."

"I guess I'll head on back," Scarecrow said.

"Take Slocum with you. Make sure he earns his pay."

"You sure you don't want one of us to stay with you?"

"I look like I need a baby-sitter, Crow?"

"I didn't mean that. It's just that, you know, hell . . . you took a pretty good spill. I just thought . . ."

"Take Slocum with you," Hardin repeated.

Slocum stared at Hardin for a minute, then shrugged. Let the ungrateful bastard do what he wanted, he thought. He walked back to his horse and swung up into the saddle. This time, he didn't bother to look back, moving off ahead of Scarecrow. The hair on the back of his neck tingled, as if Hardin was staring at him hard. Or as if someone had him in his sights and was debating whether or not to pull the trigger. Maybe, he thought, they were one and the same man. For reasons he didn't pretend to understand, Hardin didn't like him. That was plain enough.

But two could play the game, Slocum thought.

And Slocum played to win.

If Clay Hardin wanted a fight, all he had to do was push a little harder.

Just a little.

3

Slocum sat on his horse, staring at the huge house. Bigger than anything he remembered from Georgia before the war, it looked as if it had been thrown together from a dozen different buildings, each from a different era of architectural history. For a moment, it seemed to catch fire, then he realized it was just the rising sun suddenly fractured into a hundred pieces, each glittering in a different window.

He slid off the horse and wrapped the reins around an ornate hitching post of intricately carved oak. As he approached the front staircase, a broad affair of wide steps, each looking larger than the next, and the smallest seemingly a half acre, a liveried footman appeared in the front door. The footman stepped onto the broad porch, tugging at his crisp red jacket. His shoes creaked, and Slocum could almost smell the new leather.

"Mr. Slocum?" the footman asked. Slocum noticed it wasn't a question, or at least, if he wasn't who he was, the footman would have been more than a little surprised.

"Yes," he said, overcoming the temptation to pretend to some other identity.

"Mr. Stuart is waiting in the library, sir."

"No need to call me sir. Just plain old Slocum will do fine."

"Very good, sir."

Slocum grinned, but the footman retained his impassive expression.

"You the butler?" Slocum asked.

"I'm sure not, sir. I am Mr. Stuart's batman."

"His what?"

"His personal attendant, sir. Whitcomb, sir."

"I see."

"Yes, sir."

"Been with Mr. Stuart long, Whitcomb?"

"All his life, sir."

Slocum nodded. This was a way of life so strange it made the late, distant luxury of the antebellum South seem positively ordinary. He had a hundred questions, but swallowed them all as the footman held the door open and waited for him to pass into the immaculate vestibule.

"You can leave your boots over there, sir."

"I'm sorry, Whitcomb." Slocum laughed. "I didn't hear that. I thought for a second you said I could leave my boots somewhere."

"I did, sir. Over there."

Slocum followed the pointing finger and realized for the first time, by the parchmentlike skin and the slight tremor, that the man was much older than he appeared at first blush.

"I don't want to see the boss in my bare feet, Whitcomb."

"The boss, sir?"

"Yeah, you know, Mr. Stuart."

Slocum took a seat on a low wooden bench and tugged off his boots. Whitcomb offered to assist him, but that was pushing things just a little too far. When the boots were off, Whitcomb took them and extended a pair of soft leather slip-ons. Slocum slid his feet in and stood up. They felt uncomfortable, and as he took a couple of tentative steps, he had the sensation he was walking uphill. He noticed where Whitcomb had placed his boots, and spotted two other pairs, neither of which he recognized, against the wall beside his own.

"This way, sir," Whitcomb said, and moved off before Slocum could say anything.

A pair of tall glass doors opened wide on the biggest room Slocum had ever been in. Polished wooden floors gleamed in bright sunlight streaming through a tall window at the far end. Bookshelves stretched from the floor all the way to the ceiling, nearly twenty feet above.

A huge marble fireplace occupied the center of one long wall, and a staircase swept away and out of sight in the center of the opposite wall. Several large, uncomfortable stuffed chairs were positioned around the room, and a pair of long Chesterfields, stuffed as well, made a V in front of the fireplace, a narrow gap at the tight end, just wide enough to permit one person at a time to slip through.

Scarecrow towered over his sofa, and Clay Hardin sat at one end of the other. Scarecrow nodded as Slocum clacked across the wood and stepped onto the thickest carpet he'd ever seen. Hardin scowled over his shoulder for a few moments, then turned away.

Whitcomb waited until Slocum took a seat, then vanished up the stairs as if he'd been sucked up into the sky by some silent and invisible tornado. A moment later, it was as if he'd never even been there.

. Slocum watched Hardin, who seemed nervous about something and fidgeted with his hands in his lap. The fingers kept coiling and uncoiling, sometimes intertwining, sometimes clenching into loose fists, then lying slack for a few seconds.

"What's this all about?" Slocum asked. Scarecrow shrugged and Hardin ignored the question altogether.

Hardin peered up the staircase expectantly and tapped his feet, shod in the same sort of nondescript slip-ons that Slocum wore, on the thick carpet. The soft brown leather looked out of place on the bright colors and intricate, overly busy design of the carpet.

"Nice rug," Slocum said.

"It's not a rug, it's a carpet. And it's from Persia." Slocum turned to see who had spoken and found himself staring at a beautiful young woman in English riding garb. She appeared to be rather tall, unless it was a function of her standing in high-heeled boots while he sat. Slocum put her age at around twenty.

She grinned at him, as if to say what an idiot, who doesn't recognize the difference between some rag rug on a cabin floor and a luxurious Oriental import. The look on her face was enough to tell him he had made a fool of himself, at least by her lights.

"It's still nice," he said, grinning back. "Whatever it is."

"That carpet cost nearly three hundred dollars."

"That's a lot of money for something to wipe your boots on, ma'am."

"Who are you, anyway, Mr. . . . ?"

"Slocum," he volunteered. "You must be Miss Stuart."

"You're not a complete idiot, I gather."

"No, ma'am, I'm not. But I suspect even an idiot can't have much of a problem with that one."

"Oh, and why is that?"

"Well, as I understand it, there're only two women on the spread. You're not likely Mr. Stuart's mother, so you must be his daughter."

"Very good, Mr. . . . I'm sorry, what did you say your name was?"

"Slocum, ma'am, John Slocum."

"Oh, my, you even have a first name. You must not be a genuine cowpuncher." She was grinning more broadly and looked pointedly at Hardin, who said nothing, but seemed to be rather angry.

"Never have punched a cow, ma'am."

"It's a figure of speech, I thought."

"I suppose so, but it's not something I do, and it's not something I say, either."

"Why don't you shut up, Slocum?" Hardin snapped.

"Just being sociable, Hardin. Besides, it wouldn't do to snub the boss's daughter."

"She's none of your affair, Slocum. Her father doesn't want her mixing with the riffraff."

"Which am I, Hardin? The riff or the raff? And what's the difference?"

Miss Stuart laughed out loud, and Hardin looked as if smoke were about to puff out of his ears. "Mary Alice, you ought to . . ."

But Hardin didn't get a chance to finish. Whitcomb stood at the foot of the stairs and announced Addison Stuart. He turned to look back up the stairs like a man admiring a tall statue. Descending out of the gloom at the top of the staircase came the highest boots, of the smoothest leather, Slocum had ever seen. For a long moment, it looked as if the boots were alone on the magnificent stairway but there were, indeed, legs above the rolled leather tops, and a rather severe-looking gentleman set atop them.

Without ceremony, but not without self-importance, Addison Stuart crossed the room, his boots squishing on the thick pile of the carpet, and marched between the two Chesterfields to take a carefully calculated position directly in front of the massive fireplace.

"Gentlemen . . ."

"Morning, Mr. Stuart," Hardin croaked.

"Mary Alice, that'll be all."

"I want to stay, Father."

"No need. I can handle this rather well, you know. Done it before. Will do it again, too, unless I'm sadly mistaken."

"Father . . ."

"Leave us!" The voice, all gentility and reserve a second before, cracked like a bullwhip in the high-ceilinged room, echoed from the four corners almost as harshly, then disappeared, the way the sound of an unexpected slap comes and goes almost before anyone becomes aware that an angry palm has met a defenseless cheek.

Stuart watched the young woman stalk up the stairs. His three employees did the same, though not with the same purpose. Slocum could barely control his delight. Stuart caught him smiling.

"You must be Mr. Slocum," he said.

"That's me, Mr. Stuart." He stood and extended a hand. Stuart looked at it with a strange expression, as if Slocum had just offered him a rotting fish, then tilted his head a little farther back.

Slocum got the point.

"I want an explanation of what happened yesterday afternoon. And I don't want any sugar-coating. I want the plain, unvarnished truth. Clay, why don't you tell me what happened?"

"Well, Mr. Stuart, we was off to the east, open range, you know, rounding up some strays. Crow and Slocum here, along with Russ Higgins, were branding. I needed Crow to help with a bunch of beeves, so I took him with me. While I was gone, at least"—and here he paused to glance at Slocum—"according to him, Russ run down to get a few strays that got spooked."

"Is that right, Mr. Slocum?"

"Yes, sir. Russ ran them in a circle."

"Then what?"

"Well, I..."

"Not now, Slocum. I want to hear Mr. Hardin's version of events. You can fill in whatever details he leaves out. Essential details, anyway."

"Somebody jumped Russ. We lit out to see what happened. Slocum, here, got to him first. He was already dead, shot three or four times."

"By whom?"

"By Lincoln Brewster, Mr. Stuart."

"Now hold on," Slocum said, "you don't know that."

THE WYOMING CATTLE WAR 21

"I asked you to wait your turn, Mr. Slocum."

"But..."

"I saw him clear as day. He must have been lying in them bushes all afternoon, just waiting for a chance to drill somebody. It could as easily been me or Crow, or even Slocum, here."

"And you're sure it was Lincoln Brewster?"

"No doubt in my mind."

"Very well." Stuart turned to Scarecrow and, without addressing him directly, asked, "Do you have anything to add?"

"No, sir, Mr. Stuart, I don't. Clay told it all."

"I gather you don't completely subscribe to Mr. Hardin's version of events, Slocum. Is that correct?"

"It sure as hell is!"

"I don't appreciate that sort of profanity in my home, Slocum. Now, what do you disagree with? Russ Higgins *is* dead, isn't he?"

"He is, yes."

"And he *was* murdered, was he not?"

"Yeah, he was. But I'm not so sure Lincoln Brewster killed him."

"Are you acquainted with this Brewster person?"

"No, sir, I'm not."

"Then how can you say whether it was he who was responsible?"

"Because I got as close as anybody to the man who did the shooting, and I couldn't identify my own father at that distance."

"Is that true, Clay?"

"No, sir. Slocum stayed with Russ for quite a spell. We was pretty close for a while. But Brewster started to pull away before Slocum caught up with us. Then my damn horse broke a leg, and that was the end of it. But I would swear on a Bible that it was him."

"Thank you, gentlemen," Stuart said, clasping his hands behind his back, for all the world as if there were a fire in the fireplace. "That'll be all."

"But . . ." Slocum sputtered.

The response was abrupt and pointed. "Good *day*."

4

Stuart was gone with a squeak of polished leather. Hardin glared at Slocum, then rose and stalked out of the room.

Scarecrow shook his head. "Shouldn't have done that, Slocum. You don't want Clay Hardin on your ass, if you know what's good for you."

"But he couldn't have identified anybody at that distance, and you know it."

"I'm not saying he did or didn't. In fact, I'm not saying anything. And if you know what's good for you, you won't say anything more than you already did."

"I can't stand by and watch him accuse somebody for no reason."

"It wasn't for no reason. Russ is dead. That's all the reason he needs. More than that, that's all the reason Mr. Stuart and his friends need."

"What are you talking about?"

Scarecrow shook his head again. "I'm not talking at all, remember?"

Scarecrow unfolded his endless limbs and got to his

feet. A moment later, without another word or a backward glance, he too had disappeared into the vestibule.

Slocum followed him, wondering what the hell was going on. As he entered the vestibule, he saw Hardin outside, already stalking across the front yard and rounding the corral fence. Scarecrow tugged his boots on wordlessly, not even bothering to acknowledge Slocum's presence.

When he stood, he handed his slip-ons to Whitcomb, who waited silently by the front door. Taking the slip-ons in one hand, he pushed the front door open with the other. "Thank you, sir," he said, and waited for Scarecrow to step onto the porch.

Slocum dropped to the bench with a puzzled frown. He eased out of the slip-ons and accepted his boots from the ever-vigilant Whitcomb.

"How long have you been here, Whitcomb?"

"I've been with Mr. Stuart all my life, as I told you, sir. And with his father before that."

"I don't mean that. How long have you been here, in Wyoming?"

"Three years, sir."

"Anything going on I should know about?"

"I'm sure there is, sir. But I don't know what it might be."

Slocum glanced at the footman. The slightly curled lip, the old man revealing just enough of a smile to tell Slocum he did, indeed, know something, was reminiscent of the same sort of tantalizing enigma he'd seen so often on the faces of black slaves in the big plantation houses back in Georgia. It had always made Slocum feel more than a little foolish to run smack up against that kind of knowing look. It made him feel like some grand secret was being kept from him.

And it still did.

He handed Whitcomb the slip-ons and stamped his heels down into his boots. As he stepped out onto the porch, he hesitated. "Whitcomb, you know, sometimes

THE WYOMING CATTLE WAR 25

you can protect your master too much. You understand that, don't you?"

"I do, sir. Yes, I do." He shrugged. "But one does what one has been trained to do, Mr. Slocum. What else is there?"

The door closed, and Slocum peered through the polished glass as Whitcomb dematerialized back into the shadows of the house and then was gone. Slocum eased down the broad stairs and walked slowly toward his horse. Hoofbeats in the distance caught his ear, and he spotted Scarecrow on the far side of the corral, kicking up dust on his way back out to the branding corral.

Unlooping the reins from the fancy post, Slocum coiled them in his fist and grabbed a stirrup. Balanced on one foot, he almost tripped when he heard the voice.

"Mr. Slocum?"

Mary Alice Stuart stood on the top step, her hands on her hips.

"Wait a minute, would you please?"

Slocum lowered his foot and waited while she descended the stairs and crossed the yard toward him. She took her time, as if the sun wouldn't move until she got where she was going. She crossed behind Slocum's mount and stood there, smiling.

"What's so funny, Miss Stuart?"

"You are, Mr. Slocum."

"Oh?"

"You're not like the others, somehow."

"What others?"

"The hired hands."

"You mean the cowpunchers?"

"Don't make fun of me, Mr. Slocum."

"I'm not, ma'am. Just teasing. There's a difference, you know."

"See, that's what I mean."

"Life's too short, Miss Stuart. What can I do for you?"

"My father's a very powerful man, Mr. Slocum. I think you should know that."

"Money'll do that, Miss Stuart."

She shook her head. "No, that's not what I mean. I mean powerful, not wealthy, although he is that, too."

"What's your point?"

"I heard what you said in there. About Clay Hardin."

"And?"

"And I think you should be careful. Very careful."

"Why's that?"

She didn't answer him. Instead, she stepped a little closer and put a hand on his arm. Slocum looked at the delicate fingers, the snow-white skin, the careful manicure of the tapered nails. They, too, reminded him of other young women, with other powerful fathers.

"I have work to do, Miss Stuart." He pulled his arm free, against the sudden pressure of her insistent fingers.

"I think you should be careful."

"You already said that. I'm always careful, Miss Stuart. That's how I've managed to live so long."

"You're not that old, Mr. Slocum. And everybody dies. Sometimes when they least expect to."

"You're not one for plain speaking, are you?"

She looked up at him, and he realized he'd been right. She was tall. The oval face, its eyes like two bright stones in the light bronze of her skin, was framed by a tangle of reddish-brown hair that highlighted her freckles. She was tall, and she was pretty. More than that, she was gorgeous. And something told him she was trouble. Powerful fathers seemed to do that to their children. And despite playing dumb, he had no doubt that Addison Stuart was very powerful indeed.

"Anything else, ma'am?" he asked.

She turned and walked back to the house, taking each step even more slowly up than she had on the way down. At the top of the steps, she turned and looked back at him. He expected her to wave, but she just stood there a moment, arms folded under her generous breasts, then spun and pushed open the door.

Slocum wondered where Whitcomb was, but let it slide. He climbed into the saddle and started off toward

THE WYOMING CATTLE WAR 27

the day's branding. A trailing stand of cottonwoods, a windbreak to protect the big house from the worst of the weather, wound down toward the valley floor, and Slocum slowed to let his horse pick its way through.

"Slocum, I want to talk to you, cowboy."

Hardin stepped out of the trees.

"What about?"

"Never mind. Just get down." Hardin's right hand moved toward his hip, just slightly, but enough for Slocum to get the meaning.

"I think I'll stay right here, Hardin, if you don't mind."

"Get off the goddamn horse, Slocum."

This time, he let his hand settle, silent as a cloud of dust, on the butt of his Colt .45. Slocum shrugged. He eased out of the saddle, landing lightly on his toes, as Hardin stepped toward him.

"What's on your mind, Hardin?"

"I don't like being called a liar, Slocum. Not by anybody."

"Then don't lie, Clay. It's pretty simple, really. You tell the truth, nobody calls you a liar. I learned that a long time ago."

"You never learned to mind your own business, though, did you?"

"Look, I don't like what happened to Russ. I'd like to see the man responsible swinging from a cottonwood. But I don't know who that might be. And I don't think you do, either."

"I said I saw Linc Brewster. That's who I saw, and that's who killed Russ. What more do you need to know?"

"I just want to be sure, that's all. And right now, I'm not."

"Mr. Stuart's satisfied. I think you should be, too."

"You told him what he wanted to hear. That's what I think. And I don't know why, but I also think you know exactly what you're doing."

"Damn right. Brewster and some of them other nesters

are ruining the range. They don't belong in cow country. They sure as hell can't get away with bushwacking one of my men. As far as I'm concerned, anybody who sticks up for them ought to dance the same dance, from the same damn tree."

"You talk to Brewster?"

"No, I didn't talk to him. I don't have to talk to him. He done it and I know it. That's about all there is to it. If you know what's good for you, you'll go along with the program."

"What program is that, Clay? What do you plan on doing, lynching everybody with less than ten thousand acres? Takes a lot of trees, and a lot of rope."

"I plan on doing what's right."

"Sure you do."

"I'll tell you what I'm going to do, Slocum. As soon as Larry gets back from Cheyenne, me and him is going to have a little chat. Then you are last week's newspaper, Slocum. I already told him he shouldn't have taken you on. I figure he'll listen, this time."

"You about through, Clay?"

"Not quite. You best stay away from Miss Stuart. Mr. Stuart don't like her fooling around with the men."

"You have a low opinion of Miss Stuart, Clay. That's not exactly gentlemanly."

"I have a low opinion of you, cowboy. You try to poke her, and I'll have to see you don't poke anybody else. Ever."

"*Poke* her? Clay, I'm really disappointed in you. I thought you were just a louse, but I see you're even worse than that. You're a snake."

Hardin moved fast. But Slocum was faster. He slipped the punch as Hardin charged forward, then stuck out a foot as the angry foreman rushed past. Hardin landed hard and Slocum was on him. Locking an arm around Hardin's neck, he yanked his head up out of the dirt.

"Now you listen, Hardin. Larry Holt hired me to do a job. As far as I know, that was with Mr. Stuart's blessing. And I know that job didn't include putting up with your horseshit. I expect you owe Miss Stuart an apology, and I sure as hell know you better steer clear of me until you can think straight."

He let Hardin go and backed off, ready for the worst. Hardin straightened up and dusted himself off. Without turning, he said, "I'm not done with you, Slocum. Not by a long shot."

"You better be."

Slocum climbed back into the saddle. He waited for Hardin to move into the trees. The clop of hooves caught his ear and he turned to see Mary Alice Stuart sitting on her roan mare.

This time, she waved.

5

As Slocum neared the branding corral, he saw a swirl of dust spewing high into the air, like a column of smoke. The pillar moved slowly across the valley floor far below. Just ahead of it, a knot of horses, maybe half a dozen, charged across the dry earth. As the approaching band drew closer, he heard men's voices, an assortment of whoops and hollers, and he watched as a single rider, just a little ahead of the main body, slanted toward the left. The rest of the horsemen swung in a wide semicircle and fanned out.

One or two of the pursuers fired pistols in the air, and Slocum kicked his own mount into a charge down the gentle grade. As the gap closed, he recognized the lone rider as Luke Bradley, one of the temporary hands, hired on a few days before him. Luke's horse was kicking up so much dust, it was hard to see through it to the pursuing riders.

Three more shots spewed smoke straight up, little sticks of gray-white against the beige cloud. Luke leaned over his mount's neck, almost burying his face in the whipping mane, and lashed the exhausted beast for all he was worth. One of the wing riders spotted Slocum charging downhill and reined in. The others seemed to realize something had happened and reined in their own mounts without knowing quite what was going on.

Slocum angled across the face of the slope and intercepted Luke's line of flight. Luke pulled up, nearly falling from the saddle. He was bleeding from one shoulder and gasping for air. His shirt was ragged and smeared with a mixture of sweat, dust, and damp cow shit.

"What the hell happened, Luke?" Slocum asked, grabbing the other man's reins.

"Jumped me, a pack of 'em," he gulped, half swallowing his words. "I thought I was done for."

"Who the hell are they?"

"Bunch of damn farmers. Shouldn't even be out here."

"You wait here, Luke," he said, handing the reins back and wheeling his horse toward the arc of laughing farmers.

Slocum plunged back through the buffalo grass, pulling up almost nose to nose with the man in the center. "Gents," he said, flicking his hat brim with a fingernail. "What can I do for you?" Slocum looked at the big man opposite him. Sun-reddened face and fists like knuckled hams, he was almost a caricature of the Georgia redneck Slocum left far behind him. A chest thick as a hogshead pushed at his shirt, and the buttons seemed on the verge of yielding. Lank blond hair stuck out from under the brim of his hat.

When he spoke, it was with calm assurance. But the voice was not unfriendly. "You can't do nothing for us, cowboy. Question is, what can we do for you?"

"Alright, then, why don't you just tell me what that might be?"

"We can save your life, if you know how to pay attention."

"I do..."

"Then listen to me, cowboy. You tell that damn Englishman or Scotsman or whatever the hell he is to keep his cows off our land."

"And who might you be?"

"Name's Brewster, Lincoln Brewster."

"John Slocum," he answered, sticking out a hand.

Brewster seemed confused for a few seconds, then, like a man more used to shaking hands than waving a clenched fist, grabbed Slocum's in his own and shook it with stiff formality.

"Slocum, wish I could say I was pleased to meet you, but if you got anything to do with Stuart, I can't say it."

"I work for him, if that's what you mean."

"Then you tell the rest of his hands, and Stuart himself, we're tired of having our fences knocked down. We got our own herds, small ones, and we're trying to raise some crops. We don't need every damn cow in Wyoming tramping through the fields and running our own cattle off."

"Sorry about that. You boys brand your beeves?"

"No need for that. We keep 'em fenced in. That is, when Clay Hardin and his goons don't cut the damn wire."

"What's your beef with Luke Bradley?"

"Who?"

"The man you just about run to death over there." Slocum smiled, crooking a thumb over his shoulder.

"Oh! Him... well, we caught him and two others with a pair of wire snips, over by Luke McConnell's farm."

"And?"

"We run him off, just like we told him we would the last time we caught him. Next time there won't be no running. He comes back, tell him to bring his own shovel."

"That what you told Russ Higgins?"

"Who?"

"Russ Higgins. One of our hands got himself killed yesterday. Well, not exactly. He had help."

"That wasn't none of our doing."

"That's not what I hear. I hear you're the one who shot him."

"That's a damn lie! Whoever told you that?"

"Doesn't matter."

"It sure as hell does matter. Man's entitled to know who calls him a murderer. Even in Wyoming."

"Maybe so, Brewster. Maybe so. You out this way yesterday, too, were you?"

"No, I wasn't. Not that I have to answer any of your damn questions."

"Where were you, then?"

"Matter of fact, I was down to Clearwater, sittin' in Doc Wilson's chair." Brewster opened his mouth and stuck a blunt finger into a gap between two of his upper teeth. "Man's a savage. Like to pull my jawbone right out through the gum."

"Mind if I have a chat with Doc Wilson?"

"It's a free country. Go anywhere you damn please. Do whatever the hell you want. Just keep them damn cows off my land. That goes for these fellas, too. Right, boys?"

The other men mumbled agreement, but it was less than spirited. Whatever else he was, it was clear that Lincoln Brewster was the spokesman, even the leader, of the aggravated small ranchers and farmers.

"I'd appreciate it, and I know Mr. Stuart would too, if you'd not mess with any of our men. You have a problem, why don't you talk to Larry Holt?"

Brewster snorted. "Minstrel show's comin' next month, Slocum. Maybe you ought to hire on. They could use a good comedian."

"I'm not joking."

"Then you're crazy. Stuart's the cause of all this. Hell, you know it better'n I do. Damn foreigner comes out here with his big money and thinks he can buy anything he wants. Thinks he owns the whole damn territory. Him and them other stock grower types. But you can tell him for me he don't own Linc Brewster, and he don't own my land. There's only one way to get his hands on that. He knows what it is, and he knows he better not try."

"Why's that?"

"Slocum, you're a card. You purely are." Brewster wheeled his horse and lit out at a gallop. The others fell in behind him, one or two glancing back over their shoulders. One even ventured to shake a clenched fist, now that he was moving away from Slocum.

It was beginning to look less and less like Clay Hardin had told the truth. But instead of clearing the muddied waters, all Lincoln Brewster had managed was to stir them up a little more. The man was a hardhead, and his sense of himself wouldn't permit him to meet Slocum halfway.

And the more he thought about it, the more he thought Brewster might be right about Stuart. Each man was unyielding in his own way. Neither of them seemed inclined to listen to the other with an open mind. And if Stuart was half as greedy as Brewster suggested, there wasn't much chance Slocum could do anything to prevent a collision.

As he watched Brewster diminish in the distance, Slocum wondered just what kind of snakes inhabited the den of pit vipers he found himself in. He made a mental note to have a little chat with Larry Holt as soon as he returned. Shaking his head, more in sorrow than in confusion, he pushed the little chopper into a tight circle, then nosed uphill toward the corral. The big sky overhead, the bright sunlight, and the endless sea of grass should have brought a smile to his lips. At its finest, Wyoming was God's final draft, the best he could come up with for the kind of man who wanted to live by his own set of rules. The kind of man John Slocum was.

Hardin was pacing back and forth when Slocum reached the pile of rocks where the fire ought already to be blazing. He ignored the foreman and slipped to the ground. Without a word, Slocum grabbed an ax to chop some kindling. Nesting the broken slivers, he lit them with a match, then cross-hatched a few layers of slim branches. When he was satisfied the fire had taken a secure hold, he turned to Hardin, who was leaning against the nearby fence, arms crossed and lips pursed.

"Took your sweet time getting here, Slocum."

"Had some business to look after."

"It wasn't Mr. Stuart's business, I'll bet a bundle."

"Pay up."

Hardin snorted. "Slocum, I'm telling you one more time, you don't get paid to hang around. You work for your money on this spread. Every single man in this outfit pulls his own weight. No pull, no pay. It's that simple. I'm already going to make sure you get docked a day's pay. You fuck up again and I'll kick your ass out of here so fast your boots'll wonder where you went."

"Whatever you say."

Slocum turned to the heavy logs and started to lug them in twos and threes to the fire. Stacking a dozen or so alongside the rock firewall, he fed three in, placing them at an angle to let the flames lick up from the underside and start the bark burning. When the sap started to bubble and drip from the sawed ends, he arrayed the half-dozen branding irons, sticking the business end into the fire and propping the heavy steel rods against a rock.

"You seen Luke Bradley this morning?"

Slocum waited.

Finally, Hardin, curious, took the bait. "No I ain't. Why?"

"Ask him whose business I was on."

"I just might do that."

"Maybe you'll learn something."

Hardin slapped his gloves against an open palm, as if debating whether to say anything. Slocum bored in.

"By the way, I had a little chat with Lincoln Brewster a little while ago."

"What the hell were you doing talking to him?"

"He happened by. I happened to ask him what he was doing yesterday. It was interesting."

Hardin seemed nervous now. "What did he say?"

"He said he had nothing to do with what happened to Russ."

"And you believe him?"

"I don't know what to believe. But I thought Mr. Stuart might be interested in what he had to say."

"Keep out of it, Slocum."

"Look, I'm new here. But that doesn't mean I walk away from what happened to Russ Higgins. Where I come from, a man in your outfit is like a brother. Somebody hurts him, you hurt. And then you hurt back. An eye for an eye, Hardin. That's how it works. Especially with bushwhackers."

"I told you to let it be. Don't mix in this. I can handle Lincoln Brewster."

"Somehow I doubt that. Brewster didn't strike me as a coward."

"You calling me a coward?"

"Nope. Just saying Brewster won't push. You lean on him, he'll lean back. And I already told you what I think of your eyewitness identification."

"It's my word against his."

"Not anymore, it isn't."

"What are you talking about?"

"Brewster's got an alibi."

"Who?"

"I don't think it's fair to tell you that."

"I guess it's easy to tell whose side you're on."

"Hardin, I have to tell you . . . one of these days, we're going to put all this polite conversation aside and get down to business. When that day comes, you're going to see one happy Georgia boy."

6

Slocum hated riding line. And when the line was as long as the one around Addison Stuart III's Westminster Ranche, the chore was worse than usual. Hardin had prevailed on Larry Holt, going to the manager behind Slocum's back and convincing him that Slocum was too good a hand to waste on branding a bunch of yearlings.

For some reason Slocum didn't quite fathom, Holt had agreed, telling Slocum himself. Holt was a master of delegating authority, and it was unusual for him to handle such a matter personally. Slocum wanted to ask Holt about it, but had swallowed the question at the last minute. Getting away from the cantankerous foreman might be a way to keep his job. It was one he needed, and as much as he hated the new work, he was determined to hang on long enough to see Hardin lose a round or two.

The Ranche—and Stuart was adamant about the unnecessary "e"—was so big, Stuart himself wasn't sure just how much acreage he really owned. Riding the line took two days for a full circuit. If he found some fence where it didn't belong or some stray from another spread, it took longer still. Tearing out the fence was easy enough, if no one took a shot at him. Driving the strays off was another thing altogether. It took more time than it was worth, more than Slocum wanted to give it.

By the third morning, it was beginning to wear a little thin. He still had nearly fifteen miles to go on the first circuit. Unfamiliar with the route, he kept referring to the rough map Larry Holt had drawn for him. The landmarks were marked by imprecise crosses, and the water, the lifeblood of the Ranche, received prominent display in a thick double line of carpenter's pencil.

The only thing to be thankful for was the weather. Stuart still hadn't gotten around to putting up any line shacks, and in the winter, the ride would be brutal. Slocum doubted he'd be there that long, but that didn't stop him from commiserating with his successor on the line.

He watched the sun finish rising, then kicked his fire out, stomping on it and dumping the last of his coffee on the embers. Like most experienced range hands, the only thing he dreaded more than a stampede was a prairie fire. Get caught in the wrong place, and you would be little more than a barbecued side of beef, well done at that.

Losing the grass could kill a prosperous spread and most of its cattle in a single sweep across the open range. Farther south, from the Rio Grande all the way up through the southern panhandle, it wasn't that much of a problem, because the grass had enough time to grow back. But in Wyoming and Montana, there was never time for the dry grass of the late summer and early fall to regenerate. It would take until the following spring, and by then, with nothing to graze on, even a herd that managed to escape the flames would be decimated twice over and more.

He'd seen it once, the rotting carcasses, bloated with the spring thaw, stretching for mile after mile, thousands of dead cattle. At twenty-two or twenty-three dollars a head, it was a fortune, turning to gangrenous muck on the bone, the buzzards thick as rain clouds settling down over the putrid meat.

That was something he hoped never to see again.

A notch or two above Clay Hardin, maybe, but the gap wasn't that great.

Slocum had insisted on keeping the chopping horse, and Holt, against his better judgment, had agreed. That was another reason Slocum felt Holt had reasons he was keeping to himself. A bigger, stronger horse was usually in order, but Slocum had grown attached to the animal and felt as if it was the one piece of sanity in a crazy quilt with a tartan motif.

Giving the ashes a final kick, he covered them with dirt and saddled his horse. The little stallion seemed to enjoy the weight of the tack and stood easy while he inserted the bit and slipped the bridle on. His bedroll and saddlebags, heavier than normal with the tools of the line rider clinking inside the old leather, completed the outfit, and he climbed into the saddle.

Checking the map one more time, he started the final leg, hoping he could get all the way in without seeing a single steer. Chasing down a loner was tedious work. Checking the brand almost always meant that he had wasted his time or, worse yet, that he'd found extra work for himself.

The Clearwater branch of the Powder River lay just beyond a low hill to the west, and he headed up and over the crest of the hill to pick up the bank. Stuart's land followed the Clearwater almost all the way in, and he could tuck the map away for the last time.

High overhead, he heard a sharp cry, and he looked up to see a golden eagle plummeting toward the earth, its sharp talons extended like the gnarled fists of an arthritic old man. The bird nailed a rabbit on its first pass and climbed almost immediately. The horse followed its head down to the thin line of trees following the Clearwater, and Slocum relaxed, letting the reins hang over the saddle horn. Gripping the horn with one hand, Slocum let his body respond to the rhythm of the animal's stride, rocking gently in the saddle and feeling the closest thing to peace he'd experienced in almost a month.

The sound of the river had a mesmerizing effect on him, and he nearly missed the noise. It was distant, a painful bellowing, as if something were trapped and calling for help. He heard it, but it didn't register for a few minutes. Far to the east, drifting on a warm breeze, it rose and fell, blending in with the sound of the river.

When he finally realized how unusual it was, he stopped to listen more closely. For nearly a minute, he heard nothing, then the wind shifted and it was crystal clear. There was no mistake. Somewhere away from the river, cattle were blaring some sort of resentment. He nudged the horse uphill, away from the river, and eased into a trot. A narrow brook snaked downhill, and the horse took the bottom route up through a notch, then slowed, despite the prodding spurs.

The sound was sharp and unmistakable now. Still distant, but impossible to misinterpret. From the sound of it, he was listening to several hundred beeves. He pushed the pony into a gallop, scanning the ridge ahead for any sign that might explain the sound. Stuart's cattle were open-range animals, but it was not likely that so many would have gathered together in one place. They tended to drift in small groups, almost as if they were parceling out the rich grassland equally among themselves.

There was the chance, of course, that the steers didn't belong to Stuart at all, but they were on his land. Either way, it meant a headache, and Slocum had had a bellyful of those.

Two miles away from the Clearwater, the ground got a little rockier, the grassland gouged and broken, as if a giant harrow had raked across the rolling hills and sharpened gentle valleys into rock-ribbed ravines. He followed the sound and found himself climbing into the rocky hills as if drawn by a magnet.

Climbing the steepest slope yet, he reined in on the edge of a small canyon and jumped from the saddle.

Moving as close to the edge as he dared, still holding onto the reins, he slipped in among a scattering of boulders. The rough lip of the red rock canyon looked like one half of a grimace. Across the canyon, the eastern rim, equally contorted, completed the ugly mouth.

Leaning out over the lip, he peered down nearly two hundred feet. Among trees sprinkling the floor of the ravine, cattle milled and bellowed, scraping the dry earth with their hooves. He couldn't see the other end of the ravine, and the trees and brush gave him only sporadic glimpses of its floor, but even a rough guess put the number of cattle in the hundreds.

Slocum backed away for a moment and pulled the binoculars from his saddlebags. Training them on a small clump of cattle, he checked their sides as best he could. Of the dozen flanks he saw, not one bore a discernible brand. Turning the glasses on their ears, he noticed no earmarks. At that range, even through the glasses, he couldn't be certain, but he was almost willing to bet a closer look would show him nothing to change his mind.

That he would have to get closer was a foregone conclusion. He draped the glasses around his neck and backed away, tugging the reluctant chopping pony away from the brittle rock rim far enough to make mounting a safe proposition.

He nudged the horse through the sprinkled boulders, some of them massive, three and four times taller than he was in the saddle, others less imposing but more numerous, making the footing tricky. It took nearly a half hour to negotiate the descent, then he had to circle back in toward the mouth of the ravine.

Pushing through a clump of pin oak and scraggly alders, he nearly lost his seat when the horse balked unexpectedly. Twice, he tried to urge it forward, and twice, it shook its head, snorting its objection. Jumping down, Slocum tethered the pony and jerked his Winchester out of its boot.

He nearly tripped over the obstacle, banging his knee painfully on the thick split-rail gate. From either anchor post, barbed wire ran off into the brush. Slocum whistled silently, his breath hissing between his teeth and pursed lips. The cattle were not there by accident. That much was clear.

But whose were they?

And who had put them there?

The two questions raced each other around the inside of his skull, like two pigs in a circular track.

If he were lucky, he'd know the answer to the first in a matter of minutes. If not, he could be in for a long, puzzling afternoon. He got a rope on one of the larger animals, a two-year-old, by the size of it. It had been around through a minimum of three roundups, and its side was as blank as a new piece of paper.

One by one, he checked a dozen young steers. And one by one, the questions mounted. Not a single animal bore a brand. Most had earmarks, but they weren't Stuart's swallowtail or any of the other local marks he'd seen. Some didn't even have that much. But those that were marked showed all the signs of having been cut more than once.

Slocum jerked his rope off the last animal and coiled it thoughtfully, glancing up at the rimrock from time to time. There was no innocent explanation for any of it. Cattle strayed once in a while, even by the hundreds. But the odds against nearly a thousand beeves congregating together in a narrow canyon, not one with a brand, were beyond calculation. And there did not yet live the steer who knew how to build a fence.

He didn't want to be the one to carry this news to Addison Stuart.

But no one else could.

7

Slocum ignored the line and headed straight for the ranch house. The closer he drew, the harder he pushed the tired pony. He couldn't shake the feeling that the sequestered cattle meant something more than just somebody rustling a few strays and hiding them. The altered earmarks seemed somehow significant. The old cut and the new one, half overlapping, obscured the original well enough. All he could be sure of was that the mark had been altered. But in his heart, he knew the old mark had been Stuart's swallowtail.

It was hard to imagine a rustler so meticulous, and so monomaniacal, that he preyed on a single brand, yet every head Slocum examined had the identical mark. Not a single one bore a brand of any kind, and not a single one was a range maverick. The steers were all too young to have drifted any distance. They almost certainly belonged to Stuart.

The ranch house loomed up ahead, almost black against the darkening sky smeared with orange and deep pink. The clouds, high-mounded cumulus, drifted slowly across the horizon, turning deeper and deeper shades of purple, like recent bruises. The long uphill climb sapped the chopper's remaining energy and he started to slow down like a ball rolling up a steep incline.

Bright light burned in the west wing and spilled out onto the manicured lawn. Slocum didn't bother with ceremony, riding right to the foot of the front steps and letting the exhausted pony nibble at the thick carpet of grass beside the steps. He charged up to the front door and rapped sharply. He could hear the vehemence of his knock bouncing off the nearby walls and come back to him from the interior of the house.

He was already halfway through the front door when Whitcomb came down a short flight of steps to intercept him.

"Don't get in my way, Whitcomb. I have to see Mr. Stuart."

"I'm afraid he's busy, sir."

"I don't care. Either you bring him out, or I go in and get him myself."

"But, Mr. Slocum, he's entertaining important guests."

"Whitcomb, I guarantee you, there's not a more important guest in this house at the moment than me." He stepped around the old man, reaching out with one hand to brush off the feeble clutch at his sleeve. "You better show me the way, if you don't want me really making a scene."

Whitcomb was trembling. He backed away from Slocum, one hand held before him, and gave a faint wave. "Very well, sir. This way."

Whitcomb moved slowly down a long hall, lit faintly by a single lamp on a dark wooden table. The old man's shadow wiggled on the opposite wall as he moved past. One hand brushed the edge of the table, and the lamp jiggled. The shadow seemed to magnify Whitcomb's trembling, then Slocum was past, and his own shadow obscured the old man, who moved slowly, looking back over his shoulder at the demon behind him.

A pair of high walnut doors, their hardware glinting even in the dim light, blocked their path. Whitcomb reached up and knocked with a single knuckle. The tiny tapping was nearly inaudible, and Slocum stepped past him. He rapped sharply on the right-hand door. The booming of his fist exploded in the tight confines of the hall and rumbled in the room beyond the door.

Slocum heard an irritated rap of heels on the floor, and the door swung open with a rush of air. Light spilled out and Clay Hardin, reduced to a silhouette by the bright glare behind him, stared at Slocum.

"What the hell are you doing here? You're supposed to be riding line."

"I have to see Mr. Stuart."

"About what?"

"What is it, Mr. Hardin?" The burr of the Scotsman rolled around the *r* in Hardin's name, and Slocum could hear another set of heels on the floor.

"It's nothing, Mr. Stuart. Just one of the hands."

"What the bloody hell is he doing interrupting us?"

"I was just telling him that, sir."

Stuart himself materialized behind Hardin, slightly smaller than the foreman, but a far more imposing presence. "Who is that?" he demanded.

"It's Slocum, Mr. Stuart. We met the other day."

"So we did. What do you want?"

"I have to talk to you."

"Can't it wait, man?"

"No, sir, it can't."

"Well, come on in, then." Stuart placed a thick hand on Hardin's shoulder and pulled him aside, making room for Slocum to enter the room. The bright light made him blink as he crossed the threshold, and he waited a moment before he could see clearly.

A massive oval oak table, big enough for twice the dozen men seated around it, occupied the center of the huge room. A sideboard, draped in white linen, groaned under a weight of food and drink. Two big ashtrays, both full of smoking cigars sending gray wisps coiling up toward the ceiling, sat, one at either focus of the ellipse.

As his eyes adjusted, Slocum scanned the faces of the men seated around the table. He recognized only Larry Holt. The other men clearly were prosperous, even wealthy, and Slocum realized he must have been face-to-face with the majority of the local Stock Growers' Association. But the biggest surprise came when he recognized the one person not seated around the table. Somewhat removed, but clearly involved, a lap desk braced across her knees, Mary Alice Stuart gave him the only smile.

"Now, what is so important, Mr. Slocum," Stuart began.

"I think we should talk in private, Mr. Stuart."

"Nonsense. I have no secrets from these men. If it involves the Westminster Ranche, it is of concern to my friends as well as to me."

"Alright, if that's what you want," Slocum said. He hesitated, clearing his throat and trying to frame his approach. "I was riding line the last couple of days." He nodded at the ranch manager. "Larry Holt asked me to take it over."

"And you're unhappy with the assignment, is that it?"

Behind him, Hardin laughed.

"No, sir," Slocum continued. "That's not it. This morning, I found something I think you should know about."

"Well, out with it, man. What was it?"

Slocum paused again to scrutinize the faces arrayed around the table. Without exception, they were turned his way. Two or three of the men leaned forward, as if to make certain they didn't miss a syllable. One man even held his cigar suspended halfway between ashtray and lip, frozen by his intense concentration.

"I found a ravine. It wasn't on the line."

"Then what the hell were you doing there?" Hardin snapped.

"Let him talk, Clay," Larry Holt said.

Hardin glanced at his immediate superior, started to say something, then let it go.

"I was on the last leg, and I heard something. Cattle."

"Good God, man! In cow country? What a surprise!" Slocum glared at the joker, a fat man whose shirt ballooned out toward the edge of the table, even though he leaned well back in his chair.

"With all due respect, I'm talking to Mr. Stuart, not to you. I'd appreciate it if you'd shut your face until I'm done."

The fat man blubbered and started to get to his feet, but Addison Stuart waved a conciliatory hand. "He's right, Matt. Let him finish."

"They were your cattle, Mr. Stuart. I'm not sure how many head, but I'd guess seven or eight hundred, at least."

"My cattle, you say?"

"Yes, sir."

"Were they branded?"

"No, sir. But they had your earmark. Or at least they used to, until somebody overcut them. Yearlings and two-year-olds, I think."

"Not strays, Slocum?"

"No, not strays. I'm certain of that. They were fenced into the ravine. Somebody's been collecting them, for a while it looks like, and tending them. There's some grass in the ravine, but not a lot. I expect they must be herded out to graze every few days, then run on back into the ravine."

"And who do you suppose is responsible, Mr. Slocum?"

Shrugging his shoulders, he said, "I have no idea."

"You're new around here, aren't you, Slocum?" It was the fat man Stuart had called Matt.

"That's right, I am. Why?"

"Seems kind of strange. A new man, finding a ravine he supposedly don't know about. Full of another man's beeves. Just seems strange, kind of."

He puffed on a cigar almost as fat as he was. Smiling

like a cherub, he blew a couple of smoke rings that seemed to spin in the air like bicycle wheels before drifting up toward the ceiling.

"If you're trying to imply something, I wish you wouldn't," Slocum snapped. "If you have something to say, just say it."

"Oh, no, I was just thinking out loud, that's all."

"Doing a damn poor job of it, if you ask me."

"I'm sure it's just coincidence, Slocum. Damned interesting, though, don't you think."

"I think he ought to haul his ass out of here, that's what I think. I think he ought to be fired. Now!" Hardin said.

"Nobody asked you what you thought, Hardin. I don't imagine anyone would want to make you work that hard," Slocum said.

Larry Holt laughed, but said nothing. Slocum was without a single ally, and he knew it.

Hardin took a step and Slocum turned, just in time to duck the main force of Hardin's sucker punch. Moving in tight, Slocum nailed him with a combination, a left hooking into Hardin's gut and a right cross cracking into the jaw. Hardin staggered back, caught himself for a moment on the table edge, and sat down hard.

"Nice punch," Matt said, laughing. "I expect you may have boxed your way out of a job."

"That he has," Stuart snapped. "I won't stand for that sort of thing in my home. Get your gear and get off my land. Now."

Slocum nodded. "Alright."

"No! It's not alright."

Stuart stared at his daughter in amazement. "I don't recall asking your opinion, lassie."

"Well, you have it. Mr. Slocum's done nothing wrong. You let that bully abuse him, then he gets punished for defending himself. It doesn't make sense. And it's not fair."

"I'm a fair man, Mary Alice. You know that."

"Not if you let Mr. Slocum leave."

"But..."

"You ought to thank him. He didn't have to tell you what he found. Most men wouldn't. And if you go through with this, the next man sure as hell won't."

"Your language, lassie. I dinna think it's right for..."

"You dinna think, period," Mary Alice snapped, mocking his thickening burr. "If you did, you'd see I'm right."

"If anybody ought to be fired, it's that bully, there..." She pointed at Hardin, just beginning to come around. He rubbed the point of his jaw and tried to get to his feet.

Stuart seemed uncertain. "What do you think, Mr. Holt?"

"I think Miss Stuart is right. I think we ought to look into what Slocum's found. There's still the matter of Russ Higgins and Luke Bradley. Maybe it's the same people behind all three."

"Do you think so, Mr. Holt?"

"I think it's possible. I don't know Slocum that well, but he's a good worker, and I don't know anything against him. As far as Matt's two cents, I think it's about as good as Confederate money."

"You're the manager, Larry. But I want an end to this. I want to know who's been rustling my cattle and shooting my men. Hardin, here, says it's Lincoln Brewster and his friends. It probably is. But I want it stopped, and I want it stopped now." Waving a hand to take in the entire company, he said, "We all do."

The men mumbled agreement, and Stuart turned to Slocum. "I want you to help Mr. Hardin up. And I want you to shake hands. After that, I want no more of this. You work for me, you have to work together. I won't have it any other way. If you can accept that, you can stay on. If not, well..."

Slocum glanced at his right hand. He reached down

and Hardin backed away, preferring to haul himself up with the assistance of the table.

Only Larry Holt and Mary Alice Stuart seemed to notice.

And Slocum.

8

They were on the move at first light. Slocum took the lead with Holt and Hardin bringing up the rear. Stuart had been adamant. He wanted both his manager and his foreman along, and Slocum wondered whether Holt was there to ride herd on the shaky truce between him and Hardin.

By the time the sun was a full disc balanced on the edge of the eastern hills, they had settled into a steady trot. Slocum had had to change horses. The chopping pony was just too spent to recover in a single night. He felt uncomfortable on the new mount, but the muscular chestnut moved surely and easily, barely breathing hard under the easy pace, even on the uphill climbs.

They were close within two hours, and Slocum pulled up to let them move alongside. Looking at his companions, he felt like a dime novel book between expensive bookends. This little expedition was depriving the spread of its two most knowledgeable men. Not that concern wasn't warranted. Anytime somebody is stripping your herd of nearly a thousand head, you stand to lose a substantial piece of change.

And the Wyoming climate was anything but tranquil lately. One man was already dead, and Luke Bradley, although not badly wounded, would not be able to work for at least another week. But beyond the real loss was the larger crime. Someone had chosen to defy what little law there was, and shatter an all-too fragile order. Slocum doubted it was Lincoln Brewster, and in a way, he hoped to prove it in the simplest way possible—finding the guilty man.

"How much farther, Slocum?" Holt rolled a cigarette while he waited for the answer. Deftly, with one hand, he tilted his tobacco pouch, dumped a little too much into the paper, curled it, and ran his tongue over the gummed flap. The result was a little oddly shaped, but smokable, and he popped a match with his thumbnail, sucking the first smoke in and exhaling with a satisfied sigh.

Slocum pointed through a narrow gap between a pair of buttes. "About a mile, right through that notch."

"Good place for an ambush." Holt grinned.

"We can skirt it if you want. It'll add another mile or so, but it might be worth it."

"Hell no. I got too much work to do already. Let's take a look, and we can decide what to do once we get there."

"You're the boss."

Hardin hadn't said a word, and waited for Holt to fall in behind Slocum before taking up the rear. The big chestnut spooked a little as Slocum kicked it through the gap between the two huge red slabs. The stratified rock looked like wood grain, or a stack of thick papers, each layer jutting out as if to call attention to itself, to let an observer know he was not looking at a monolith.

Slocum glanced up when a few loose rocks skittered down the steep face of the right-hand butte. The horse danced sidewise as the rock clattered over a sloping fan of loose scree, then regained his form when the sound died. The buttes met at an angle, each heading in a different direction on the far side of the gap. The land beyond was full of fractured slabs of the same red rock, and a few chimneys of some harder stone jutting up from the valley floor like petrified trees or monuments to Lot's wife.

The ground sloped uphill, and stray cottonwoods, rooted where the wind had dropped their seeds, vied with ragged brush and weedy clumps for the sunlight and rain. Ten minutes through, Slocum pointed again, this time not breaking stride. "There's the mouth of the ravine, right where that line of trees cuts across our trail."

"That where you found the fence?"

"Yeah. Pretty well concealed, too."

"Say again what brought you here in the first place."

"I could hear the cattle. They were spooked by something. I figured it must have been a catamount. I didn't see it, but something sure had them worried. Behind the fence, they had no place to go but back and forth. The ravine isn't that long, and it's closed at the far end. If a big cat got down in there, he could choose his own steak."

"Well, we'll have them beeves out of there in jig time. Hell, less than a thousand, we maybe could drive them out ourselves, then send somebody out to give us a hand."

"I don't know about that," Hardin said. His voice cracked from disuse, and he coughed to loosen it. "A thousand, that's a lot of beeves, Larry."

"Hell, Clay, we ain't goin' to Chicago. It's fifteen damn miles. What kind of wrangler's scared of a cakewalk like that?"

"I ain't scared. I'm just saying maybe we ought not to jump too quick. Like Slocum says, we don't know how them cows even came to be here. Anybody around, we might wish we had more help."

"Hardin's right," Slocum said. "It won't be easy."

"Maybe I should have left you ladies home." Holt laughed again, but Slocum had the distinct impression the manager wasn't kidding.

At the trees, Slocum dismounted. He moved in, looking for the gate. He'd misjudged the spot by several yards, found the gate, and opened it. Walking back to his horse, he felt the hair on the back of his neck stand on end. He stopped in his tracks and listened for a long moment. The cattle milled around, but they seemed strangely silent. Something was in the air, but he couldn't put his finger on it.

Shaking it off, he stepped out of the trees and climbed back into the saddle. "This way, gents," he said, spurring the chestnut's flanks and rocking with the big stallion through the undergrowth.

Holt followed him, Hardin again brought up the rear. Once inside the ravine, Holt let out a long whistle. "Jesus, Slocum, you weren't whistling Dixie. Get a rope on one of these damn cows, and let's see what we can see."

Slocum jerked his lariat free and opened a good-sized loop. He nailed one of the frightened beeves on his first toss, jerking the rope tight and holding it while Holt dismounted. The manager followed the rope in close, one hand curled around the tight line, the other patting his thigh.

When he got close enough, he reached out to slap the cow's muzzle. The blow wasn't hard, but it seemed to settle the animal down. It looked at Holt, its great brown eyes wide and motionless. Holt grabbed an ear and leaned toward it, rubbing the edge with a gloved thumb.

Letting the ear fall back against the cow's skull, he ducked under the rope and circled the animal. He kept well out of reach of the hooves as the cow swiveled its head to follow him. "Damn!"

"Well?" Slocum said.

"You sure as hell were right. That's an overcut, and a damn good one. I saw that mark once, seven, eight years ago, down in the Texas Panhandle. It wasn't local there, either. I don't know..."

"And no brand, right?"

"Right... no brand."

"What do you think?"

"I think you just might be right about Brewster. No damn nester is likely to be that good. Probably wouldn't know how to mark, and sure as hell wouldn't waste all that time. No, sir, this is somebody knows beeves and ranching. Somebody who's been around. That ain't Brewster."

"You don't seem surprised."

"I ain't. Never did buy that story, Slocum. I think old Clay is just trying too hard. Ain't that right, Clay?"

Hardin ignored the jibe, sucking on his teeth and staring off at the rimrock. "Whatever you say, Larry."

"Slocum, you go all the way down the other end of the ravine?"

"Nope."

"Think maybe I'll have a look. You and Clay can wait here."

Hardin looked at Slocum, but said nothing. Holt got back into the saddle and poked his mount with a single spur. The horse seemed almost to jump, and a moment later he was gone.

"This don't change a thing, Slocum. You know that, don't you?"

"Hardin, why don't you just forget about it. Come spring, I'll be gone. We got six months or so, and I guess I can get through it if you can."

"I don't want to get through it. You come sniffin' around Mary Alice again, like you been doin', and you and me are going to write a finish to it."

"Hardin, don't you see how it is?"

"I see fine."

"You think so? Let me tell you, I may be new around here, but I've seen men like Addison Stuart the Third before. They're all cut from the same cloth. If you think his daughter's fair game, forget about it. The only real difference between her and most of the girls like her is that she *thinks* she's different. But she's not, and neither is her father. You and me, Hardin, we're the hired hands, and that's all we'll ever be. Hell, they don't even see us when they look at us. All they see is calluses and sweat-stained clothes. We carry the worst stink, Hardin, the stink of work."

"Mr. Stuart's been more than fair with me, and besides, I ain't always going to be a foreman. I can move up, maybe manage a spread like Westminster. Hell, maybe own one, even. But you keep trying to mess that up for me."

"I'm not trying to mess anything up. If you want to walk around with your head in the clouds, go right ahead. But stop trying to make me out to be a spoiler. I don't want anything from Addison Stuart but a day's pay for a day's work. I don't want anything at all from Mary Alice Stuart."

Hardin was about to respond when a rifle shot cracked against the walls of the ravine. Slocum instinctively looked toward the sound, but it came from every direction. He wasn't sure what was the real thing and what was the echo. Hardin looked up at the rim, then wheeled his horse.

"Where the hell are you going?" Slocum shouted.

But Hardin was gone.

Another shot cracked, and a third. This time, another, smaller weapon responded, a handgun, somewhere lower down, maybe even on the ravine floor. Slocum pushed the chestnut into a gallop, charging toward the sound of the pistol. He called to Holt, but no one answered. Another rifle shot exploded, this time much closer, and Slocum heard the rattle of an empty cartridge bouncing off the stone wall as it tumbled down into the ravine.

He called to Holt again, his voice slapping the rock like hands clapping, but Holt didn't answer.

As he raced through the scattered trees, cattle bolted in every direction. Slocum jerked his Winchester out of the boot and held it in one hand while he snapped the reins to keep the big horse moving. The rifle sounded once more, this time just above and behind him. He leapt from the horse and took cover behind a red boulder. The stone crumbled beneath his fingers as he worked his way around to the far edge. His gloves looked as if they had been long ago covered with blood now flaking away.

Lying on the sandy ground, he eyed the rim from left to right. A rock slipped over the edge and dropped straight down, landing with a crack on some loose stone directly ahead of him.

Slocum braced his Winchester against the side of the boulder and waited. He saw the hat first, a black Stetson, its brim folded into a tight curl, Texas style. The brim seemed to hover in the air without a thing to hold it up, then it tilted toward him and a face appeared.

Half a face, really, as the glimpse stopped halfway down the nose. Slocum slipped the safety off and let the front sight settle just under the hat brim. He waited patiently, but an abrupt silence descended, bringing a frozen immobility with it. It seemed as if time had ground to a halt.

Fearful the man on the rim might back away, Slocum squeezed the trigger. The brim snapped up and back away from the edge and out of sight. But not before he'd seen the new black hole just left of center in the high forehead. He didn't recognize the man, but knew they would never be introduced now.

"Holt?" he called.

"Slocum, you alright?"

"Yeah, you?"

"So far..."

The next shot sounded different. Higher up and from farther away. Slocum spotted the small cloud of gunsmoke sifting down into the ravine. He fired twice, and the slugs ripped at the red rock, showering fragments back down into the canyon. The whine of the ricochets died, and Slocum felt a chill. It was too silent.

"Holt?" he shouted. "Larry? You okay?"

9

Slocum staggered under the weight of the body. Holt was a small man, but he was compact and solidly built. Straining to lift the body onto the horse, he wondered about the coincidence. He'd been here the day before, and the place was deserted. He hadn't even seen a sign of human presence, except for the fence. A day later, men had lined the rimrock, obviously waiting. He wanted to believe Hardin was responsible, but there was just no proof.

Too many people knew he'd discovered the ravine. There was no lack of candidates for the fly in the ointment. It was true the cattle were all Stuart's, and that made Hardin a possibility. Who would have better access to the Scotman's stock, and less reason to be suspected of rustling?

But raising cattle was a cutthroat business. Any one of Stuart's good friends in the Stock Growers' Association had reason to reduce the competition, rake off a few choice steers, and pocket a nice piece of change.

You could weaken Stuart and enrich yourself at the same time. Those were both powerful inducements.

And, as much as he hated to admit it, Hardin had logic on his side, as well. Things in the Clearwater basin had been simmering for a long time. The cattlemen hated the small ranchers, the farmers, the sheepmen. The animosity was like a poison, and it had penetrated every aspect of the basin's rudimentary social life. Livelihoods were at stake, and so was a way of life. Any man hardy enough to make a living in the Clearwater basin was not likely to be deterred by murder, if he felt he had no choice.

With the corpse finally draped over the saddle, Slocum tied it securely in place. He looked at Holt's hands, dangling almost to the ground on one side of the horse, and wondered at how easy it was to reduce so vibrant and powerful a man as Larry Holt to a slab of undressed meat. And Slocum knew, even as he tried to dismiss the thought, that Holt was not the last victim, only the latest. Hardin and Stuart were certainly going to demand revenge, Stuart because he didn't like being crossed, and killing his manager was an insult to his influence, Hardin if for no other reason than to preserve his protective veneer of righteous indignation. But he had run away, just when the shooting started, and that was going to take some explaining.

It wasn't over by a long shot. And Larry Holt had seemed to be the only man willing to be reasonable in the face of the inexplicable. Making matters worse, Slocum was now without an ally in the Stuart outfit. Holt had hired him, and Holt had defended him. Now Holt was dead.

Trailing the reins of the dead man's horse in one hand, Slocum climbed into his own saddle. He tied the reins to the back of his saddle and looked up at the bright red rock towering above him. The cattle had settled down, and lazily munched stray clumps of grass as if nothing had happened. In a way, nothing had. Whatever had led him here had not changed. The men responsible were still alive, still able to continue their plans, whatever they might happen to be. Only Larry Holt was dead.

Slocum clucked to his mount, and the big horse started at a walk, jerking against the bit a little, trying to set his own pace. Slocum held him back out of concern for Holt. He knew it was foolish, but it didn't seem right to go galloping out of the ravine as if he'd just heard Cookie's triangle clanging for chuck.

He looked back once or twice, then turned his face resolutely for the mouth of the ravine. Hardin should be halfway home, if he went straight there, and Slocum was not looking forward to his own arrival. The sun was brighter than usual, the air a blue that seemed almost thick, the few scattered clouds drifting through it accenting, deepening the color.

As he rode, it occurred to him that the attacks on Russ and Luke might not even be related to what had just happened. He'd only gotten a glimpse of the man who killed Russ Higgins, never even saw his face. But the dead man lying behind him on the ravine floor was not the same man, of that much he was certain. Nor was he a farmer or a small rancher. He didn't stink of sheep, and that meant only one thing—he was a hired hand or he was a flat-out rustler. When they brought him in, somebody would know if he belonged to one of the local outfits.

An hour later, he saw the small cloud approaching him and steeled himself for what he knew was coming. The cloud thickened, boiling up behind a half-dozen horses running flat out. Hardin must have yanked some hands from the roundup and sent them back to help out.

Too late for Larry Holt, he thought. And when he considered it, he wondered whether Holt had been an accident. What if the dry-gulchers had been waiting for him? Suppose whoever tipped them, or gave them their marching orders, had expected Slocum to be the first in? Was there a personal element that he couldn't figure? The question chewed at him, and he kept swatting it away, trying to concentrate on the approaching riders.

But it wouldn't go away.

As the riders grew closer, Slocum recognized Scarecrow at the head of the pack. He reined in and waited for the men to cover the last quarter mile. They urged their horses on even harder, kicking up swirls of dust and ragged grass. Scarecrow nearly fell from his horse when he finally tugged on the reins to slow his mount down to a walk.

He covered the last few yards in a trot, then sawed the reins again. The horse protested, his gums peeling back as he gnawed at the steel bit. "You alright?" Scarecrow asked.

Slocum nodded.

"Killed him, did they?"

"Yeah. He got one and I got another one. Never seen either one of them before."

"Why don't you go on in. I'll stay with Larry's body. Hardin's sending a buckboard. I guess we can throw them other two in as well, long as we keep 'em separate. Don't seem right, somehow, bringing a dead man and the men who killed him home in the same wagon."

"You sure?"

"Yup. Luke'll stay with me. These other fellows'll drive them cattle out of the ravine. I guess we better brand them up. Then we got some work to do. Somebody's got to pay for this. Hardin says he already knows who."

"You know he's wrong about Brewster, don't you?"

"Yeah, I know it."

"He say why he hightailed it when the shooting started?"

"Nope. Only said something bad happened. Said he was up top when Larry got hit, and he knew you and Larry needed help."

"You buy that?"

"Never buy what I don't need."

"Aren't you going to say anything, Crow?"

"What's the point? If I knew who done it, I maybe could convince Hardin he's wrong. But I don't know how to take the only candidate away from him and give him nothing in exchange."

"It's not him, either, is it? It's Stuart."

"You're almost right. It ain't Mr. Stuart, either. At least, not just him. It's all of 'em. Slocum, they got money and they own about every lawman and politician for five hundred miles. You been around, and you know what that's like."

"Crow, you have to say something. Brewster is innocent. Suppose Hardin or one of his cronies kills him?"

"Larry was innocent, wasn't he? Somebody killed him. It happens, Slocum. You know that. And besides, maybe Brewster is responsible. He don't have to be the one who killed Russ to be mixed up in all this. One thing I do know, though."

"What's that?"

"Unless we start shooting back, more of us is gonna get shot. We got to draw the line. It don't even have anything to do with them cows. Not anymore. It's about who we are. We got to stand and fight."

"Even for the wrong reason?"

"Hell, Slocum, you're a reb. You'd know more about that than I would."

Slocum ignored the taunt. Things being what they were, it was as like as not that Scarecrow himself had worn gray. But there were certain realities that one learned in that war that were lessons hard learned. And they were lessons that ought to be remembered if one didn't wish to learn them all over again, just as hard.

"Where's Hardin now?" Slocum asked.

"Said he had to do some gettin' even. I expect he's going to have a talk with Lincoln Brewster. If he can find him. If not, well, old Clay is a mite excitable. He'll probably lean on one of them nesters, just so he feels like he done something."

"He go alone?"

"Clay ever do something alone?"

Slocum smiled at the sarcasm. He shook his head slowly, then reached back to untie the reins of Holt's horse. Handing them to Scarecrow, he said, "Appreciate it. I owe you one."

"I'll collect, don't worry."

Slocum dug his spurs in and the big chestnut, unencumbered by the drag of a second horse, jumped into a full gallop. Clearwater was nearly ten miles away, and Hardin had a good head start. He wanted to get there before Hardin, but that was next to impossible. The next best thing was to hope the big settler wasn't around. But like most of the small ranchers, he seldom strayed too far from home. Working their own land seemed almost a religion with them. Slocum remembered his attachment to his own family land, and envied them a little, but this was one time when that attachment might bring more trouble that it was worth.

Behind the western mountains a huge thunderhead spiraled up out of nowhere. A great blue-black column, it flattened its head against the sky, spreading out like a strand of clay hit with a two by four. The cloud started to mushroom, and a herd of other, darker clouds seemed to follow in its wake. In five minutes, the sun was blotted out almost completely.

A few blades of brilliant white stabbed out in every direction, but they vanished one by one as the cloud mass thickened and settled into a uniform gray blanket. The lead clouds scudded low over the mountains, running downhill like frightened mustangs. They hid the peaks a few moments later and rushed toward him like a living thing.

By the time he reached the town limits of Clearwater, the first few spatters of rain slapped his hat brim and left silver dollar–sized spots on his shirt and dungarees. The horse seemed to sense something and jerked its head, fighting the reins. Slocum wondered whether it was the coming storm or something more dangerous, and less visible, in the air.

He thought he'd try the Double Eagle on the off chance Hardin had stopped for a little liquid courage. The saloon was almost empty.

Mac Gilray, the barkeep, nodded as Slocum pushed the swinging double doors open. "Slocum, what'll you have?"

"Clay Hardin been here?"

"Left about twenty minutes ago."

"He liquored up?"

"A little. No more'n usual, though."

"He say where he was going?"

"Nope. Seemed like he was in a hurry, though. Say, he told me about Larry Holt. Damn shame. You and Larry are about the only men in the whole Clearwater basin knew when you had enough. The rest of the fools around here is drunks or teetotalers. Ain't got use for neither kind. The one gives me no business, the other gives me more than I need."

Slocum ignored the philosophy for the idle chatter it was. "Which way's Linc Brewster's spread?"

"West end of town. Linc's not in, though. He stopped by early, day before last. Said he had to go clear to Cheyenne for something. Be back tonight or early tomorrow."

Slocum thanked him and backed out through the doors without turning around. It might be time to have that little chat with Doc Wilson, he thought.

The dentist had an office a few doors down from the Double Eagle, and Slocum found it without much trouble. He climbed the steps two at a time. On the landing, he stood with his back to the street and rapped on the door. Trying the knob, he pushed the door open and stepped inside. It was dark inside, and he could hear a strange hissing sound, like steam escaping through a valve.

"Doc?" No one answered. "Doc?" Slocum called again. The hissing continued, but there was not another sound but his own breathing in the gloomy waiting room.

Slocum pushed on into the dental theater, where it was even darker. Taking another tentative step, his boots slipped on something wet on the floor. Slocum fell heavily, landing on his right shoulder. He lay there a moment, trying to get his breath, then struck a match. He found himself watching the small flame and a pair of its twins. The light danced in Doc Wilson's dead eyes.

A bone-handled knife lay on the floor beside him, still loosely gripped in curled fingers, where Wilson had jerked it out of the deep wound in his chest. Blood seeping from the wound had already started to coagulate.

Brewster's alibi was useless now.

10

Slocum closed the door quietly. Part of him wanted to call the sheriff, and part of him wanted to leave the Clearwater basin behind as soon as he could. As cruel as it seemed, he had no choice but to leave the discovery of Doc Wilson's body to someone else. Unsure of himself, and conscious of Stuart's influence, he couldn't afford to get involved. Clearwater was too full of contradictions, its people too volatile. Already, he wished he'd never heard of the place. Its residents seemed determined to cut one another to ribbons, and leaving was starting to look like a good idea.

He walked back to the Double Eagle and mounted up. The Brewster spread was the only place left to go, and he let the horse have its head. As Clearwater fell away behind him, the rutted road curving away and uphill, he glanced back once. The town was strangely silent, almost as silent as Doc Wilson's office.

Up ahead, against the pale gray sky, a plume of oily black smoke suddenly erupted. As he rode toward it, it spread out in every direction, surrounding itself with a dark gray pall. Slocum pushed the horse a little harder. He knew the old saying about smoke, and lately there was plenty of fire. The only question this time was what might be burning. If things ran true to form, it would be the Brewster place. But if Mac Gilray was right, at least this time there'd be no dead body. Brewster could thank his stars. Another spatter of rain slashed at him.

The wind picked up, and the clouds scudded by ahead of it. Faint patches of blue started to appear, then a bright, hot sun ballooned through the clouds and the threatening storm was just a memory. Maybe it was a good sign. Maybe things weren't as bad as they seemed.

But Slocum was wrong. He broke over a ridge and saw the column of smoke coiling up from a burning barn. The roof was already gone, and as he started downhill, its great cross beams collapsed inward, sending geysers of orange sparks spiraling up on the superheated air. The walls were sheets of flame, and sticks of hay, carried by the air currents, spun crazily in the air, every once in a while catching fire, then darting still higher as black ash.

The sign at the entrance to the hard-packed dirt lane read Shaughnessy. Slocum heard gunshots as he reached the open gate and pushed the horse on through. A small clump of frightened sheep mewed in an unearthly chorus as they shrank against a fence, their yellow wool speckled with blood where the barbed wire tried to keep them back.

The lane curved to the left, and Slocum took it at a fast gallop. Expecting the worst, he yanked the Winchester loose and levered a shell into the chamber. He could see one end of a big log house, its chinks wattled with mud. The horse shied away from the crackling flames and the near wall suddenly gave way, peeling away from the beams and landing with a thud. A wall of heat slammed into Slocum as he galloped past and broke into an open yard of baked clay.

Hardin, at the head of a knot of men all of whom held weapons, turned as Slocum dismounted.

"What the hell are you doing here?"

"I was about to ask you the same thing, Hardin."

"Getting even, Slocum. I figure I'll start at the bottom and work my way up to you."

"Better quit while you're ahead, Clay."

Hardin kept tilting off center, first one way, then the other. Each time he corrected the imbalance, he overcompensated. His speech was slurred, and his eyes looked glassy. It didn't take a doctor to see he was drunk.

"You set this fire?"

"Sure I did, so what?"

"Shouldn't have done it."

"Then make me put it out." Hardin's hand wavered uncertainly over his gun butt. The cowhands with him started to slide away, as if they wanted no part of what was about to happen. But Slocum didn't want to kill the man, at least not in the shape he was in. It wouldn't be a fair fight, and besides, he told himself, Hardin is somehow the key to everything. He either knows what's going on, or knows someone who does.

"Go on, Slocum, go for it."

Slocum shook his head. "Nope, not today, Hardin. Two things I never shoot, fish in a barrel and drunks. Right now, you're both. Too easy."

As if in response to the insult, a rifle shot cracked, and the slug slammed into the baked clay, kicking up chunks hard as pebbles and scattering them over Slocum's boots. The men scattered, and Slocum hit the deck, just ahead of a second shot.

He waved his hat in the air. "Hold on," he shouted. "Hold your fire."

Another shot slammed into the ground scant inches from his head. He tugged a kerchief from his pocket and waved it as high in the air as he could. Hardin, his face buried against the ground, kept mumbling, but it was incoherent and Slocum started to wonder whether the man had lost his mind.

Slowly, to make certain the shooter knew he was not

attempting to charge the house, Slocum got to his feet. "Hold your fire," he shouted again.

"Why should I?" the voice shouted back.

Slocum walked toward a horse trough hard up against a low shed attached to the barn. He grabbed a bucket from a peg in the wall and scooped it full of tepid water, then hurled the water onto the shed roof. "Give me a hand, you men," Slocum shouted, turning to the pack of Hardin's cronies, most of whom stood stock still, as if they had been flash frozen.

"Come on," Slocum snapped. "You started it, you put it the hell out. Now!"

"But Clay won't..."

"The hell with Clay. I don't give a damn about him. Give me a hand or by God I'll shoot every last one of you."

Something in his voice told them he meant it, and Scarecrow broke rank first. Walking toward Slocum with both hands extended, like a blind man feeling for a wall, he stopped about two feet away and took a second bucket. Backing away, he stopped in front of the well pump and started to crank, letting the bucket sit until the first spurt of water gushed out, then he kicked the pail in place and pumped faster.

"Come on, you guys, give me a hand."

Slocum finished dousing the shed roof, and replaced Crow's bucket with his own. A second man joined him, then a third. Clay Hardin sat up and rubbed his eyes, for all the world like an infant waking from an afternoon nap. The men worked quickly now, passing three pails back and forth and working on the burning walls of the barn. It was too late to save the main building, but they had to stop the flames from spreading to the shed and possibly jumping to the house.

When the last few flames were doused, Slocum let the pail fall from his hands and wiped sweat away from his eyes, licking at a few stray drops on his upper lip. His lungs hurt, and his arms ached from the furious pitching of the heavy oaken pail.

Hardin had collapsed into a heap, and lay curled in a ball, with his head cradled on one arm. Grabbing the pail again, Slocum filled it one last time and lugged it over to where Hardin lay. He hefted the pail by its handle and tilted it just enough for a trickle to slosh over the rim. Directing the cold water carefully, he watched as Clay Hardin started to uncurl, spluttering as the water ran into his mouth and nose. When the drunken foreman started to sit up, Slocum doused him with the rest of the water.

Hardin cursed and scrambled out of the way, but too late. He was soaked through. Slocum hauled him up by the shirtfront and shook him furiously. "You bastard. Why?"

Hardin tried to jerk free, and when he saw that he couldn't, he reached for his gun. Slocum saw the hand groping desperately for the pistol butt and beat him to it, snatching the heavy Colt from its holster and holding the muzzle right under Hardin's nose.

"You bastard," Hardin spat. "You son of a bitch. You're fired. I'll have your ass for this, Slocum. You can't get..." But Slocum's fist cut him short. Landing right on the point of his chin, it knocked the foreman back a half step, but Slocum refused to let go of Hardin's shirt. He jerked him forward again, ready to land another punch, when a door banged open.

Slocum stopped and looked toward the house, where a woman in dungarees and a checkered shirt stood on the step-up porch, a Springfield repeater braced on her hip.

"Stop it!" she screamed. "Stop it, stop it, stop it! Haven't you done enough damage? Do you have to kill one another before this is over? Do you?" In frustration, she jerked the carbine to the side and fired a shot into the air. "Get off my land, all of you! Go back where you belong, please..." In the last, there was a note of desperation.

The woman was right, and the men seemed to understand that. Almost sheepishly, they walked toward their horses, glancing back over their shoulders as if to be certain she didn't plan to shoot them down one by one, then climbed into their saddles. They were gone in an instant, leaving Slocum and Hardin alone under the thick pall of smoke slowly beginning to dissipate ahead of the quickening breeze.

Hardin glared at Slocum as he tried to twist his way free, but Slocum wouldn't yield, and the shirt came away with a shriek as it split down the back and peeled off his arms. "Damn you," Hardin hissed.

Slocum tossed the shirt at him and turned away. He started toward his horse when he heard the Springfield levered and cocked. He turned back to see Hardin raise his hands slowly, the Colt in one muddy fist.

Touching the brim of his hat, Slocum said, "Thank you, ma'am. I believe he would have shot me."

"Don't thank me. I would have let him, if I'd had time to think."

"Neighborly, aren't you?"

The woman snorted. "My last neighbors were Comanches. Guess I've come down a notch or two since then."

Hardin brushed past him, but Slocum barely noticed. His eyes were riveted to the striking woman with the deadly weapon in her hands. Her hair was wound in a tight braid on top of her head, the bright red coil picking up stray sunbeams as the last of the storm blew away.

Only dimly, he heard the sound of Hardin's horse clip-clopping down the lane and fading away.

"You're next," she said. "Git!"

Slocum smiled. "No place to go," he said. "I just got fired."

"You're luckier than my barn," she said.

Slocum nodded. "That's true enough. I'm sorry about that. I wish there was something I could do about it."

"There isn't."

"I know, Miss . . ."

But she didn't take the bait, letting the blank hang in the air unfilled. She snicked the safety on the Springfield and let the stock clunk on the porch. "I suppose I should thank you," she said. "Just a little."

"No need. You mind if I clean up before I ride out?"

She didn't answer him, instead turning and disappearing inside the house. He was halfway to his horse by the time she popped back out the door.

"I thought you wanted to clean up," she hollered.

"Yes, ma'am." He turned to see her holding a thick towel and a hunk of brown soap.

She met him halfway, tossing the towel and soap the last few feet. He caught both and smiled. "Thank you, ma'am."

She spun away and started back to the house. As she reached the doorway, she said. "There's some soup, if you're hungry." Then she was gone, leaving a faint scent of flowers behind in the smoky air.

11

Slocum cut a hunk of cornbread and smeared it with a thick layer of butter. Wiping the bowl clean, he sopped up the last drops of the barley soup and chewed the bread quietly. Maggie Shaughnessy watched him with detachment. Her son, an eleven-year-old named Brian, smiled.

"That's good bread, isn't it, mister?"

"Real good, son."

"My mom made it."

"She's quite a cook."

"She made the butter, too."

"Like I said, she's quite a cook."

"You learn to do what you have to to keep body and soul together," Maggie said, shrugging off the compliment. "It's passable butter, no more than that."

Slocum chewed thoughtfully, swallowed, and took a drink of water. "You know, Mrs. Shaughnessy, I feel real bad about what happened to your barn."

"Why should you?"

"I guess I sympathize. I mean, it wasn't my problem,

but I know those men. Most of them are decent. I don't know what got into them, why they would do something like that. Especially to a woman."

"You mean a widow, don't you?"

"No, ma'am, I mean a woman. It's not right."

"There's a lot that's not right here, Mr. Slocum. The whole Clearwater basin is not right, nor the people in it. You feeling bad won't change that, so just forget about it."

"Can't do that, Mrs. Shaughnessy."

"What are you going to do, turn the clock back and put out the fire the next time they show up?"

"Nope. But I maybe could help you build a new one."

"Oh, really? And where am I supposed to get the money for lumber, Mr. Slocum? Charity? Or are you wealthier than your clothes would suggest?"

"I think I can get the money. Seems to me Mr. Stuart owes you."

"It does, does it?"

"Yes, ma'am, it does."

"You can't get blood out of a stone, Mr. Slocum. And that man is the next closest thing. If you can get money out of Addison Stuart, maybe you can raise the dead, too. Maybe you can bring my husband back. And my brother. Maybe you're gifted, Mr. Slocum, a saint, perhaps. But even if you *could* get the money, I couldn't accept it."

"Why not?"

"That's none of your business, Mr. Slocum. Anyway, I don't want your help."

"Seems like you could use it, all the same. I'll make you a deal. If I get the money, will you let me build the barn?"

Maggie stared at him for a long time. Her piercing green eyes made him uncomfortable, as if they were boring right through skin and flesh, looking at the very bones of him. She wiped her lips with a napkin, reddening them with the scrape of the linen. Her eyes seemed to flare up with green flames for a few seconds, then as quickly as it had come, the fire was gone.

She crumpled the napkin and let it drop onto her plate. "Alright," she said. "On one condition."

"What's that?"

"That you not lie to him. You tell him exactly who the money's for, and why. If he gives it to you, you've got yourself a barn to build, and if not, a train to catch."

Slocum nodded. "Fair enough."

Maggie stood and gathered the dishes. Slocum offered to help, but she turned him down. "Save your strength," she said, "you'll need it for that damned Scotsman. They're notorious skinflints. You know that, don't you?"

"Who, the Stuarts?"

"The Scots, all of them. My family spent four years in Scotland, near Inverness, before my father could earn passage to America. Anyplace else on earth, it would have been two years, at most. But they won't let go of a farthing without an order from the Queen."

"Maybe your father drank too much..."

"My father never had a drink of whiskey in his life, he didn't."

"He's Irish, isn't he?"

She blushed, but held her ground. "Aye, he was. As Paddy's pig."

"Well, then, there you are. He drank up half the money, that's why it took you twice as long to get passage. Just like an Irishman."

"I know what you're doin', Mr. Slocum, but it won't work. Stuart is a penny-pincher, plain and simple. And a murderer into the bargain, if you ask me, and even if you don't."

"I doubt that very much, Mrs. Shaughnessy."

"A regular doubting Thomas, aren't you, Mr. John Slocum?"

"Aye, that I am, Maggie Shaughnessy."

Brian could control himself no longer. His head had been going back and forth like he was watching a tennis match. "He sounds just like Papa." Brian laughed.

"Don't you be comparing this no-good drifter to your father. Shame on you," Maggie shouted. "Shut your mouth and go to your room."

"Ma, I..."

"Go on, boy..."

Slocum watched Brian hang his head and push back his chair. Getting up slowly, the boy shuffled toward the door, staring at Slocum the whole way. When he was gone, Slocum said, "I'm sure the boy meant no harm, Mrs. Shaughnessy."

"I know what's harmful and what's not, Mr. Slocum. What he meant isn't the point at all. And I'll thank you to get out of my affairs. You're here, if at all, to build the barn your friends took from me. That's all."

"Of course. But..."

"No, Mr. Slocum. That's *all*."

"Thanks for the meal."

Maggie wheeled to face him. "And where is it you're goin' in such a hurry?"

"To see Mr. Stuart."

"I see."

"Don't worry, I'm not running out on you."

"Oh, no, I'd never be worried about that, Mr. Slocum. You're a knight in shining armor, you are. They always come back after they kill the dragon."

"Only a lady as fair as yourself would know that."

"Don't you be flattering me. Go on with yourself."

Slocum smiled, and in spite of her anger, Maggie smiled back. "You be careful, now," she said. "That Clay Hardin is a right spalpeen."

"I'm sorry...?"

"Spalpeen, a, ah, a scoundrel..."

"Oh, yes. Well, I don't think he's much of a threat."

"Not to your face, but don't turn your back on him. I'm speaking from experience."

Slocum started to ask, but Maggie, realizing she had invited an intrusion into her privacy, cut him off. "Never mind..."

Slocum walked to the door and stepped out onto the porch. His horse raised its head and flicked its mane as he stepped into the yard and approached it. When he climbed into the saddle, he stopped for a moment to look at the house. Maggie was watching him from behind a kitchen curtain. Brian, too, peered out from his own window.

Biting his lower lip, he jerked the reins and wheeled the horse in a single, fluid semicircle and lit out down the lane toward the road to Clearwater. For the rest of the ride out to the Stuart spread, he kept turning things over in his mind, trying to find the way into a locked box. No matter which way he turned it, he found no place for the key. At the long, looping approach to Stuart's house, he was no closer to a solution than when he'd begun.

Leaving his horse at the hitching post, he crossed the lawn, leaning forward a little against the slope as he climbed. On the porch, he yanked the bellpull, then turned to look out over the valley. It was a breathtaking vista, and as far as he could see, almost to the foothills of the Big Horn Mountains in the West, the land belonged to Addison Arthur Stuart III. It would have been funny if it hadn't seemed suddenly evil. Under the big sky, people naturally had big ambitions. But Slocum was beginning to think there ought to be limits.

The cattlemen had been shrewd and, in the beginning, even scrupulously law-abiding. But that had begun to change as the money got bigger and the competition fiercer. Once the land itself became an issue, the die was cast. Stuart, like so many others, had wisely used water as his anchor. Staking claims along water courses, they claimed, too, the land on either side. It gave them absolute control of the water, and the land outside the limits of their properties was much less desirable without access to the one single thing that made it possible to sustain life itself, let alone any sort of meaningful commerce.

Wrapped in thought, Slocum didn't realize Whitcomb

was behind him until the old man cleared his throat. Slocum turned and found the old man looking down his nose in a disapproving way.

"I'd heard you were no longer with us, Mr. Slocum."

"You heard right, Whitcomb."

"Then why are you here?"

"Does that mean you're not glad to see me?"

Whitcomb smiled. "Nothing new there, Mr. Slocum."

"Whitcomb, you old dog, you mean you disapprove of me."

"And others like yourself, Mr. Slocum. But I don't make the rules around here, I just enforce them."

"I need to see Mr. Stuart."

"Didn't we just go through this a few days ago, sir?"

"We did."

"Then is this a new play, or merely another act in the same tired farce?"

"You talk too damn much, Whitcomb. Take me to Mr. Stuart."

"Yes, sir."

The old man allowed Slocum to open the door himself, then led the way down the same corridor, this time stopping halfway through and knocking on a half-open door. Perhaps realizing how futile it was, he didn't make an issue of Slocum's boots.

"What is it, Whitcomb?"

"A visitor, sir."

"Show him in, show him in."

Whitcomb bowed, waited for Slocum to push the door open, then said, "Mr. John Slocum, sir."

"Slocum, that bastard, he wouldn't have the nerve," Stuart said, spinning in his chair. He banged his knee on the big mahogany desk and mumbled something inaudible.

When he saw it was, indeed, Slocum, he frowned.

"So, it really *is* you. What do you want?"

"Two hundred dollars."

"What the bloody hell for?"

"A certain lady's barn was destroyed by some of your employees."

"Too bad. But I have nothing to do with that."

"Oh, but you do."

"Slocum, I don't know what you think you're up to, but you really ought to run along. You're not welcome here, as I'm sure you can understand."

"Actually, I don't like it any more than you do, Stuart. But fair is fair. Your men burned the barn. On your orders, directly or indirectly. You ought to pay."

"Well, I won't. Not a bloody cent."

"That's what she said."

"She?"

"Mrs. Shaughnessy."

"I see."

"Does that make a difference?"

"Not in this life, Slocum. Now, get out!"

12

"You didn't get the money, did you?"

"No, I didn't."

"What did I tell you?"

Slocum didn't answer. Maggie looked at him a long moment. He felt as if he'd let her down. And more than a little wounded pride made him feel that much worse. "I guess I overestimated the man's decency."

"You can't overestimate what isn't there."

"Maggie, he's a hard man, but I think you misjudge him."

"Oh, Johnny, Johnny, Johnny. Hope springs eternal, doesn't it? But even a true believer like you must know the South lost the war. You have to go on with your life, and you've done that. Well, that's the way it is with Addison Stuart. I know what he is, and I'm prepared to go on with my life. You should do the same."

"I'll be leaving in the morning," he said, preferring not to deal directly with her insistence.

"You can sleep in the shed tonight. It's dry and it's

clean. I don't suppose it smells too good, what with the smoke and all that, but..."

"Actually, I was planning to sleep out on the flats. I can make camp down by the river."

"No need."

"Thank you, but..."

"Whatever you say, Mr. Slocum. I'm not one to twist a man's arm, or try to make him do something he doesn't want to do."

"That's what I like about you."

"You don't know me well enough to like me, Mr. Slocum. If you did, I don't think you'd like me at all."

"You're full of mysteries, aren't you?"

"Better that than bein' full of what some other folks are full of."

"That doesn't become you, Mrs. Shaughnessy."

"I'm past caring."

"Why are you so bitter?"

"Bitter? Oh, I don't think that's fair. I see things for what they are. I don't have the time for false hope, Mr. Slocum. I'm not bitter, just clear-sighted. And a little hardheaded."

"And honest, too," Slocum said with a smile.

Maggie relaxed enough to return a pale imitation. "Yes, that too."

Slocum stepped toward her and reached out a hand. She took it in her right and closed her left over the top. "You be careful, John Slocum."

"You too, Maggie. I'm sorry for all this."

"I can handle it. It'll get worse before it gets better, but..."

Slocum turned and headed out the door. For a moment, he stopped with one foot suspended between the porch and the hard ground. He thought he'd heard Maggie say something, but all he heard was a cricket in the bushes and the mournful call of a hungry owl. He mounted the chestnut, realizing it belonged to Stuart. His own horse was back in the Westminster corral. He'd have to swap horses in the morning before heading for God knew where.

The ride to the river was the longest in memory. He felt deflated, felt that somehow he had lost a fight he could have, even should have, won. By the time he reached the trees along the Clearwater, he realized he was dead tired. He made camp hurriedly, building a morning fire, filling his coffeepot and setting it beside the unlit fire, then rolling into his bedroll. He rolled his gun belt around the holster, the Colt Navy loose enough to come out with two fingers, and closed his eyes.

Another owl hooted a few times. He wondered whether it was just irritated or if it was hunting. He knew owls, because of their unusual feathers, made no noise in the air, their powerful wings beating silently and letting the predator glide through the night sky without a whisper of their presence.

But that, too, was no comfort. The night was full of enough mystery to baffle a wiseman, and Slocum just didn't have the energy to cope with any more uncertainty. He concentrated on the slight ripple of the water, the occasional splash of a frog. It was no comfort, but he was too tired to realize it. Before he knew it, he was asleep.

When the twig snapped, he wasn't sure he heard it. He lay there like a coiled rattler, every nerve alert in an instant. He strained his ears, but heard nothing. Slocum thought he'd been dreaming when another footstep snapped another dry twig. It might be a deer, but he didn't think so. If the deer knew he was there, it would have run; if it didn't, it wouldn't have tried to be so silent. Whatever was out there in the dark was trying to be quiet because it knew he was there.

For one terrifying moment, he imagined a grizzly, but it just didn't seem likely. He slipped the Colt out of its holster, squeezing the leather to keep it from moving. When the muzzle cleared the holster, he started breathing again.

His horse pawed the ground nervously, and Slocum

strained to see through the pitch-black. The new moon was no help, and the stars, big as they seemed, were nothing but distractions. The trees looked like they had been carved out of coal and spilled even darker shadows on the ground.

He had just started to move when he heard a sharp scratch, and froze in place. Among the trees, a match exploded into a wavering flame, then settled down. He heard glass on metal, and the match threw a shadow back into the woods. A moment later, a coal oil lamp, its wick turned up high, filled the small clearing with light.

It sat on the ground among the trees, and all he could see was the hat brim of the person who lit it. When she turned, he took a deep breath.

"Slocum?" she called. "Slocum? Are you here?"

She held the lamp high, and it spilled shadows down over the front of her, hiding her face in the shade of the broad brim of her Stetson.

Slocum eased the hammer back down on the Colt, but he still felt like a coiled spring. He couldn't imagine what the hell she was doing here.

"Over here," he hissed.

She screeched, a little quiet shriek, as if unwilling to wake whatever might be sleeping. He sat up and watched her swing the lantern, still not quite sure where he was.

"Right here," he said.

This time she saw him. She walked quickly, as if afraid of something that lay behind her, just beyond the reach of the lamp's small circle of pale light.

"Were you sleeping?"

"Yes, I was."

"Sorry to wake you, then."

"It's alright."

She knelt beside him, placing the lamp on the ground and rubbing her hands against the night chill. "Are you warm enough out here?"

"I've been a lot colder," he said.

"It's frightening, out here in the dark."

"You shouldn't be out here anyway."

"Maybe not. But I couldn't not come. I had to."

"Why?"

"I don't know. It's just that . . . I—felt that I wanted to . . . I can't really explain it."

"Then maybe you shouldn't have done it."

"You men, you always try to be logical. Some things don't lend themselves to that sort of thinking."

"Only women can't be explained."

She reached a hand toward his face. He thought for a moment she was going to smack him, but she settled for running the fingertips over his cheek. "You need a shave."

"And a bath."

"We could go for a swim."

"In the middle of the night?"

"Why not, it'll be fun. Come on." She sprang to her feet and grabbed him by the hand, tugging him up, then letting go. She walked slowly, almost deliberately, down through the trees. He grabbed a hunk of soap as he heard her boots crunch on the gravelly sand and he broke through the trees as she bent to pull them off one by one.

"Come on, I'll race you," she challenged. "Bet I get in before you do." She started working at her buttons, tugging the heavy shirt off and tossing it in a heap on the boots. Her dungarees came next, and Slocum couldn't believe his eyes.

She stood there, one hand coyly curled between her legs. In the darkness, her skin seemed to glow. She was a statue of bronze and shadow. She turned away, almost demure for a moment, as he slipped off his clothes. He watched her, the curve of one full breast trembling gently as she ran a hand through her hair.

When his clothes lay in a heap next to hers, she broke for the water. Slocum sprinted after her, launching himself into the air as she waded in ankle-deep water. He hit cleanly, in a shallow dive, his knees grazing the pebbly bottom, and did a few quick strokes to pull himself out into deep water. His feet felt for the bottom, and he popped up, shaking the water from his hair.

She stood there, etched against the dark woods, the water just below the shadowy V between her legs. "It's cold," she said, shivering.

"It wasn't my idea." He laughed.

"Go ahead, blame it on me, Mr. Slocum." She took another couple of steps toward deeper water, then leaned into it, letting it break over her shoulders and ducking her head just under the surface. Her long legs flashed, tossing off an arc of water that would have been silver in the sunlight, but was little more than a matte gray in the darkness.

When she surfaced, she was five feet away. The water reached just below her breasts, and she folded her arms across her chest, more to keep warm than to conceal anything. Slocum let his knees bend and sank into the water up to his neck. He rubbed furiously at his skin, then rubbed the softening soap into his hair, working it into a thin lather. Ducking to wash it away, he repeated the process and got a little more positive response from the soap.

He ducked again and came up laughing. She splashed him, and he fell to the side, dog-paddling and slashing his palm at the surface. The water cascaded over her in sheets, and she flailed her arms to protect herself. Her prominent nipples, stiffened by the cool air, stopped him in his tracks. He found the bottom and moved toward her, draping an arm across her shoulders and pulling her close. He felt the hardness of the nipples against his chest and bent to kiss her, sliding his tongue in her mouth for a brief instant. He pulled away when she nipped his tongue between her teeth.

He felt his cock stiffen, and her hand fell beneath the surface of the river, clutching at him. Her fingers curled around the length of him, stroked him three or four times, then squeezed. "Impressive, Mr. Slocum. But I didn't come here for that."

"Too bad," he said.

She collapsed in his arms, snuggling against him and

letting his cock slip between her legs. "Just hold me like that for a minute," she whispered.

He pressed himself against her, letting his hands slide down her back. Grasping her muscular ass in both hands, he lifted her, but she slithered away.

"No, I mean it, no, Mr. Slocum." She backed away, lost her footing a moment, and fell backward, landing on her rump in shallow water. He knelt beside her, but she turned away.

"Don't ruin it," she said. Her voice was hoarse and strangely distant. He watched her get to her feet. Backing away from him, no longer concerned about covering her magnificent breasts, she found the safety of the sandy shore. He waited there in the water while she tugged on her dungarees. He didn't want to frighten her, and he was more than a little embarrassed by his insistent erection. She picked up her shirt and slipped into it before looking at him again. The shirt still hung open as she walked back to the water's edge.

"Don't worry"—she laughed—"it will go down quickly in the chill."

He took her at her word, wading to shore and stepping onto the sand. By the time he reached her, he was still hard, and she reached out to let her fingers graze the length of him.

"It's a pity," she said.

He leaned forward and wrapped her in his arms. He held her close for a moment, then at arm's length. "Why *did* you come here, then?" he asked.

Instead of answering him, she reached into her pants pocket. She withdrew something and stuffed it into his surprised palm. His fingers closed over it for a moment and he held it close.

"What is this for?"

"What do you think it's for?"

"I don't have any idea."

"I'm sure you'll think of something." She buttoned her shirt slowly. He watched her in silence and felt a tremor as her long fingers slipped down inside her dungarees to tuck in the shirttails. He started to protest, but she stopped his lips with one long finger.

"Good night, Mr. Slocum."

He watched the fingers finish fumbling with the buttons, leaving only the top two undone, a tantalizing curve of solid flesh arcing away in either direction and disappearing under the heavy shirt.

He didn't know what else to say, so he nodded. "Good night, Miss Stuart."

13

Slocum sat up the rest of the night. Three times he counted the money Mary Alice had stuffed in his hand. Each time it had come to the same thing—two hundred and fifty dollars. She had offered no explanation, but he realized she must have heard him talking to her father. An hour before sunup, he lit the fire and put the coffee on, then dressed.

As usual, the coffee was bad, but it was black and strong, and it jolted him like a clenched fist. For some reason, he no longer felt the despair of the previous evening, despite his confusion. Saddling the horse, he found himself whistling, as if with the sun a whole new optimism had washed over him, carrying him along whether he wanted to go or not.

At six-thirty, he entered the lane and saw Maggie in the yard, pumping water from the well. She looked up once, then turned back to her work. The pail was full when Slocum climbed down from his horse.

"Morning," he said.

"I thought you were leaving. No need to say good-bye twice."

"Why so friendly?" Slocum grinned.

"I've said too many good-byes in my life to enjoy another one," she said, picking up the pail and turning her back on him. He watched her cross the yard, the water sloshing over the pail rim and trickling silver down her leg, leaving little pools of light behind her on the ground.

When she got to the porch she turned. "You coming in, or not?"

Slocum tied his horse to the corral and walked slowly toward her. Planting himself directly in front of her, he stopped with an enigmatic grin smeared on his face. The porch gave her a few inches, and she stared directly into his eyes. "What's so amusing?"

He opened the flap of his shirt pocket and tugged the bills free. He squeezed the wad between finger and thumb, fanning them out just enough for her to see how many there were, but not their denominations. "You know what this is?"

"How could I know that?"

"Look at it, take a close look."

"Alright, so . . . ?"

"That's your new barn, Maggie Shaughnessy." He tucked the bills in her shirt pocket and picked her up. She refused to let go of the pail as he swung her around. The water sloshed over them both, the pail finally rapping into Slocum's knee and knocking him off balance.

"You're a crazy man," she shouted. "Put me down."

"Aren't you happy?"

"Who did you kill?"

"What do you mean?"

"Last night you said Stuart didn't give you the money. This morning you carry on like you just found the end of the rainbow. You must have robbed somebody, or found a dead man with a fat wallet."

"No, nothing like that."

"Well, how did you get it then?"

"Does it matter?"

"I wouldn't ask if it didn't."

"Mary Alice Stuart paid me a visit last night." Maggie raised an eyebrow and tilted her head to one side. Then he nodded. "No," he said, "it wasn't like that. I guess she overheard me talking to her father. She stuffed the money in my hand and said I'd know what to do with it."

"I see."

"You don't seem pleased."

"Should I be?"

"Well, I thought so, yes."

"Then you're more naive than I thought, Mr. Slocum."

"Will you tell me what's going on between you and that family?"

"Nothing special. They have everything and I have nothing. They took what little we had when we came here. Now they're trying to take all the rest of it away."

"Maybe it's time to say no, put an end to all that."

"Maybe so. I'm sorry, Mr. Slocum. It's just . . . look, I know you mean well. Thank you. Maybe . . ."

"Maybe nothing. Where's the nearest lumber mill?"

"Mr. Reynolds, in town, at the hardware store, can make the arrangements."

"Let's go, then."

"It's too early. He doesn't open until nine o'clock."

"Then let's have some coffee."

"Have you eaten?"

Slocum shook his head. "Not hungry."

"Don't be silly. Let me make you some breakfast. Come on inside."

She smiled for the first time that morning, and it was the first genuine expression of pleasure he'd seen on her beautiful face.

"That's more like it," he said.

"More like what?"

"Never mind."

Maggie blushed and turned away. She carried the half-empty bucket into the house, and Slocum followed her in. She busied herself with the cookstove, then set the table while Slocum watched her silently.

Brian came into the kitchen, his hair still tousled from sleep, rubbing his eyes with closed fists. When he saw Slocum, he broke into a broad grin. "Mr. Slocum, you're back!"

"You know how to use a hammer, Brian?"

"Yes, sir. Why?"

"We got a barn to build."

"I told you, Mama. I told you he would do it."

"Hush up, Brian. Go wash up and get your breakfast."

The time seemed to move at a snail's pace, but eight-thirty finally arrived, and Slocum hustled Maggie out to saddle her horse. At two minutes before nine, they were standing in front of Reynolds Hardware and Dry Goods. Reynolds himself showed up a minute later.

"Mornin', Maggie, kind of early for you to be in town, ain't it?"

"It is Doak, it is, but I've got a lot of work to tend to. Can't get started without supplies."

"That was a terrible thing about your barn."

"That's what I'm here about."

"Maggie, I'd like to help you, but I can't do business on credit. You know that."

"Who said anything about credit?" Slocum snapped.

The storeman looked from Maggie to Slocum and back to Maggie. "Who's your gentleman friend?"

"John Slocum," Slocum said, sticking out a hand.

Reynolds looked at it warily for a moment, then shook it wanly. "You used to work for Addison Stuart, didn't you?"

"News travels fast."

"It's big news in a small world, Mr. Slocum. Anytime somebody goes head to head with Clay Hardin, folks around here kind of take an interest."

"Well, I'll tell you something, Mr. Reynolds. I've kind of taken an interest in Hardin myself. But we didn't come here to gossip. We need some lumber, nothing fancy. Whatever'll do for barn siding. Not crap, either."

"It'll take a few days. I don't stock that much without a special order. I have a shipment coming in this morning, but it's spoken for."

"Who's it for?"

Reynolds licked his lip, but didn't say anything. "Let me open up, and we'll see what we can do." He turned away and fished a key out of his jacket pocket. Throwing open the door, he raised the shades and moved to the back, where he lit a lamp.

Slocum followed him on in, despite Maggie's tug on his sleeve. "Who's the shipment for, Mr. Reynolds."

"Addison Stuart."

"He pay for it yet?"

"No, he runs an account with me. We settle up every quarter."

"Then it's not his lumber yet."

"I ordered it for him."

"Order some more. We'll take this one."

"I can't do that. Mr. Stuart would . . ."

"Would what?"

"Nothing. It's just that I . . ."

"He know it's due today?"

"No, he doesn't."

"Fine, we'll take it."

"How much do you need?"

Slocum turned to Maggie. "How big was your barn? About twenty-five by thirty?"

"I don't know. I guess . . ."

"And sixteen feet high?"

"You got that much coming in, Reynolds? And for the roof, too?"

"Oh, much more than that."

"Alright then, how much?"

Reynolds took a stubby pencil and a sheet of brown paper off a roll. He did some quick figuring. "With the beams, I figure two by sixes on that, and the roofing, I make it to be about"—he paused to lick the pencil point and make a final calculation,—"about two hundred and twenty-seven dollars. Call it two twenty."

"That include nails?"

"Yup."

"Alright then, pay the man, Mrs. Shaughnessy."

"But..."

"No buts, Mr. Reynolds. You send that lumber out to Mrs. Shaughnessy as soon as it comes in. Mr. Stuart can wait a few days. The man needs to learn a little patience."

"What if he finds out?"

"I'll handle it. In fact, I'll hang around, just to make sure you don't forget."

Turning to Maggie, he said, "You go on home. I'll be there as soon as I can."

She was reluctant to leave, but Slocum gave her a series of little shoves, and she finally surrendered to the inevitable. As she mounted her horse, Slocum stood in the doorway. "Maybe you ought to round up a few friends to give us a hand. It'll go a lot quicker."

Maggie nodded. "I hope you know what you're doing, John Slocum."

"Me too," he said under his breath. "Me too."

14

By the time Slocum showed up with the lumber, a half-dozen men were sitting on the porch. He recognized Lincoln Brewster, but the others were all strangers to him. The three wagons creaking along behind him were quite a sight as they made a wide swing to head straight through the gate. Twenty-foot lengths of one by eight hanging off the open tailgate, bowing from their own weight and snapping with the shifting wagon bed, made the horses sweat and the wagons groan.

Slocum dashed through the gate and Maggie rushed off the porch to meet him. "You did it," she said. "You really did it! I can't believe it."

Brewster got slowly to his feet and shambled toward them. "By God, you sure put one over on that bastard, Stuart. Slocum, if we had a man like you here a few years back, he never would have gotten his hooks so deep into this country."

Slocum grinned. "It's all in knowing how." He laughed.

"By God, you got that figured about right, I'd say."

"Let's get to work, then."

Slocum walked away to direct the lead wagon to a spot a few yards away from the outer edge of the blackened square where the old barn had been. Brewster and his men had already cleared away the charred remains and dragged the spot to make it level. Stakes and lines blocked the new perimeter and charred sheathing had been peeled away from the back wall of the shed. They were ready to build, and they seemed more than anxious.

One by one, the wagons were unloaded, Brewster directing the placement of the raw timbers. "No point in lugging the stuff twice," he said. "Tommy, make sure you count them boards right. Lay 'em out like I showed you and drop them beams right in place. We'll get this damn thing done today, with any luck. Randy, get them nail kegs one at each corner. Save yourself some steps, alright?"

The men took his bullying well, grinning like fools but doing what he said. "You seem to know your stuff, Brewster," Slocum said.

"My daddy was a carpenter, my granddaddy too. Them bastards had a hammer in my hand when I wasn't no more'n six or seven. Never forget it. Had a broken thumb three times before I was ten. But you know, I learned how to drive a nail. Can't beat that kind of learning, Slocum. No, sir."

When the wagons were unloaded, Brewster called the men together, even before the freight handlers had moved into the lane. "Alright, everybody. This is not going to be easy, but we can do it. And remember, we're not just building a barn for Maggie Shaughnessy. We're teaching Addison Stuart a lesson. Everybody ready?"

The men nodded their heads, starting to catch some of Brewster's enthusiasm. "Okay then, let's build us a goddamn barn!"

Working in teams, two men laid out the frame while two more started measuring and cutting the siding timbers. In two hours, the frame was up. They called Maggie from the house to drive in the last framing nail. She wiped her hands on an apron, took a step back, and swung the hammer furiously. It glanced off the nail head and left a deep imprint of the hammerhead in the lumber.

"Got to do better than that, Maggie. Pretend that nail's Stuart. Let's see what you can do." Catching the spirit, she spit into one palm and then the other, adjusted her grip on the heavy tool, and slammed it so hard, she not only drove in the nail, she countersunk it and dimpled the lumber with the force of her blow.

"Now you're talking, Maggie." The men teased her unmercifully for the next hour as she ran back and forth with lunch and coffee. Even during the meal, the men worked in teams, half eating while the other half kept on working. Slocum never stopped at all, drinking coffee on the run and sawing like a man possessed.

By two-thirty, they started on the roof. The going was a little slower, but they still pushed themselves. Brewster cracked the whip like an animal tamer, driving them beyond their endurance, pitching in whenever an extra hand was needed, working at his own piece of the project when it wasn't.

Slocum stopped to catch his breath and stood beside the big man, who was sawing timbers for the roof. "I'm expecting somebody later, Slocum. I think you ought to meet him."

Slocum shrugged. "Sure, why not? Who is it?"

"Name's Nate Holder. Ever hear of him?"

"No, should I have?"

"I guess not. Just thought you might have."

"What's he coming here for?"

"What do you think?"

"I can't guess."

"Stick around. Hand me that file, would you. Damn saw is getting dull. Green lumber, I guess." Brewster grabbed the file and swung the saw around, teeth up. "Grab that other end, if you would. Thing'll wiggle like a damn snake, otherwise."

Slocum gripped the blade and watched as Brewster

used the file deftly, honing each tooth with three or four swipes of the file.

"Can't do too much of that, you end up with no saw at all, pretty soon."

"I got to hand it to you, Brewster, you really know your stuff."

"Look, Slocum, I know you're just passing through. You don't have a stake in the Clearwater basin. The rest of these folks'll die here. Only they want somebody other than Addison Stuart to decide when their time might be. You understand what I'm trying to tell you?"

"Not exactly."

"What I mean is, it's nice of you to help Maggie out. But I don't want you filling her head with no notions. She's a good woman. Folks respect her. She works hard and she takes good care of that boy of hers."

"And . . ."

"Well, I guess what I mean is, don't take advantage of her. We're her neighbors, and we'll look out for her. You don't want to answer to us, make sure help is all you give her. And maybe you ought to plan on moving on, soon as this mess stops boilin' over."

"I was planning on that, anyway. But I assure you, I have no designs on Mrs. Shaughnessy."

"It wasn't your designs I was worried about, Slocum, it was hers. I see how she looks at you, we all seen it. Except you, probably. But it's there, plain as day."

"Don't worry about it, Mr. Brewster."

Brewster tossed the file to the ground, where it stuck in the earth at an angle. "Linc," he said, extending a hand, "that's what my friends call me."

"Alright, Linc it is. Now, who's this mysterious visitor you were hinting at?"

"Never mind. He'll be here this evening. We're having a little meeting at my place, about seven-thirty. Maggie's coming. Why don't you tag along with her?"

"Maybe I'll do just that, Linc."

"Good. Now, look out. I got some wood to cut."

Brewster bent to grab another one by eight and snapped

it like a piece of cloth so that the far end rose just high enough to clear the sawhorse, and he whipped it sidewise, letting it drop with a clatter across the supports. "Shit, where's that line? I marked thousands of these things, seems like. This one should be measured already."

He flipped the board with a twist of his wrists and leaned forward to get a better look. "There it is," he said. "Alright, Slocum, maybe you ought to get up on that roof. We still got to go some before we knock off."

"You're a hard man, Linc."

"Got to be, Slocum. This is hard country. And besides, I ain't no harder than Addison high-and-mighty Stuart the Third."

Slocum nodded, then walked to the ladder leaning against one finished side of the barn. He was halfway up when he heard a shout and turned to look back over his shoulder.

"Riders comin', a whole passel, looks like."

"Better get your gun, Slocum," Brewster bellowed, sprinting for his horse to grab his own gun belt.

Slocum scurried down the ladder and rushed to the front porch, where his gun belt was draped over the railing. He cinched it on and loosened the Colt Navy, then broke for the mouth of the lane. Brewster and two other men were already there. Both of the others carried carbines and Brewster had a Colt Peacemaker, almost dwarfing the big pistol in his huge fist.

The riders broke into the lane, coming full tilt. Brewster fired once in the air, and the lead rider reined in. It was Clay Hardin.

"You're not welcome here, Clay. Not after what you done to Mrs. Shaughnessy's barn."

"Stay out of this, Brewster. This is between me and Slocum there."

Slocum stepped in front of Brewster. "What can I do for you, Hardin?"

"I come to fetch Mr. Stuart's lumber."

"Don't know what you mean, Clay."

"I mean the lumber you hijacked this morning from

Doak Reynolds. And you damn well know that's what I mean."

"That lumber was bought and paid for. You can ask Reynolds. I got a bill of sale right here in my pocket." He reached into his shirt and fished the folded paper out.

"I don't give a damn about no paper. I ordered that lumber myself. It come in and I want it."

"Sorry, Clay. You didn't leave a deposit. I bought it fair and square."

Hardin laughed. "You don't have any idea who you're dealing with, do you, Slocum? You think this bunch of sheepfuckers is any match for me and my men? Is that what you think?"

"I think you ought to watch your language, Clay. There's a woman and young boy here. They ought not to have to hear that kind of talk. Especially from the likes of you."

Hardin jumped down from his horse. Slocum watched the twitching fingers of the right hand, drifting toward the hip, then moving away, as if Hardin didn't quite know what he wanted to do. Three other men jumped down from their mounts and fell in behind Hardin. The others sat back in their saddles, tilting their hats back as if they were getting ready to watch some kind of show.

Slocum saw Scarecrow far at the back of the pack. The man suppressed a faint smile, but said nothing. "Sorry we can't help you, Clay. Now, if you boys don't mind, we're busy."

"Don't turn away from me, Slocum. I ain't through with you yet."

He grabbed Slocum by the shirt, and Slocum spun free, turning back as one of the men with Hardin went for his gun. Slocum cleared the holster with his Colt and ducked to one side. He fired once, catching the would-be gunman high on the right shoulder. "Clay, maybe you better ride out of here while everybody's still breathing."

"Slocum, I ain't leaving without that lumber. It's rightly Mr. Stuart's, and I mean to have it back."

"Hardin, Mrs. Shaughnessy used to have a barn here, until you burned it down. That barn was rightly hers, and we're building her a new one. You can stay and help, or you can haul your ass out of here. One or the other. Those are the choices. Make yours and let me get back to work."

"You can't get away with this. There're laws around here. You'll be hearing from the sheriff."

"You looking for me?" Ray Kandel said. He stepped out from behind a corner of the barn where he'd been helping with the last few pieces of siding.

"Sheriff, this here lumber's been stolen."

"Sorry, Clay. I already talked to Doak this morning. Slocum bought it fair and square. Next time, maybe you should leave a deposit. I got a couple stray hammers here, you want to help. If not, I'll see you around."

"You'll be singing a different tune when Mr. Stuart takes your badge."

"Clay, I know Addison Stuart better'n you do. And I don't think it will make a difference to him. In case it does, though, he can come down and pick up the badge any damn time he pleases. And you can tell him I said so. I'm getting sick and tired of watching you all pick at the little people around here. You keep on, somebody's going to get hurt."

"It won't be me, Sheriff."

"Don't bank on it, Hardin." The ice in Slocum's voice put an end to the dispute. "The next time I see you, the first uncivil word I hear, and we are going to settle this thing. Unless you want to do it right now."

Hardin glared at him, but said nothing.

"Well? What's it going to be?"

Scarecrow nudged his horse forward. "Come on, Clay. Let it be," he said. Hardin stood still for one tense moment, but then he mounted up. He waited as the others filed through the narrow lane. He never once took his eyes off Slocum, and he never blinked.

Then, with a nod, he was gone.

15

Lincoln Brewster's house was packed with people. Small landholders from fifty miles in every direction crammed into the front room and the large kitchen. Everyone seemed to be talking at the top of his lungs, shouting into a neighbor's ear in order to be heard over a dozen neighbors doing the same.

Brewster himself stood quietly at one side of the huge fireplace. A small fire, more for light than warmth in the mild evening air, crackled sporadically, and Brewster leaned in now and then to add a log or poke the fire to bring it back from the edge of extinction.

Slocum, too, was quiet. He sat in a corner, watching the people work themselves up into a euphoric optimism totally unwarranted. Nate Holder had not yet shown, and Slocum wondered whether he would show at all. Brewster remained outwardly confident, but his eyes kept darting to the front door at every lull in the conversation. He was nervous, and Slocum didn't blame him. Brewster had been on the money when he'd pointed out that Slocum had no personal stake in the outcome. He could cut and run anytime he chose. Everything in the Clearwater basin that mattered to him would fit on his horse's back.

Brewster and the others, though, were in a different boat. They had too much invested. They had brought too much of themselves, too much of their former lives, too much of what they hoped would be their futures, to this valley. They had put down roots, some deeper than others. But without exception, they were fastened to the earth in a way Slocum was not.

If they were to leave, they would be tearing themselves away from everything in the world that mattered to them. They would be cutting themselves off from too much. They could not survive that sort of upheaval, not many of them could, anyway. And not a man in the house was unaware of that fact.

But Slocum had thrown his lot in with these people. There was no denying, at least not to himself, that Maggie Shaughnessy was the main reason. But she was not the only reason. Slocum felt responsible for some of what happened. He knew that some of it was his fault, and that some more of it could have been stopped if he'd been paying more attention. He hadn't been, and that, too, was his fault. The only way to atone for that was to stand shoulder to shoulder with this motley army and try to help them defend their lives and their livelihoods.

When the door banged open, Slocum felt a sudden chill. The man in the doorway looked like a lurid phantom from a fanciful bible. He might have been the devil himself. Thin to the point of gauntness, his skin almost unnaturally white, he looked at every face in the room, one by one, out of a pair of black eyes so dark and so dead-looking that it made Slocum shiver. This was a man who was not afraid of death, either his own or someone else's.

"Brewster?" he said, partly a question and partly a challenge. "I'm Nate Holder. I understand you have a job for me."

"I do," Brewster said, hesitating a moment before

moving away from the wall and slipping among his neighbors, who seemed to have been frozen in place. Brewster stuck out a hand, but Holder let it hang in the air like an unanswered question.

"Let's go outside. I can't hear myself think in here," Holder said.

Brewster nodded, throwing a look full of desperation Slocum's way. Slocum nodded and got to his feet. Holder uncoiled like a bullwhip, pinning Slocum to the air with those flat, cold eyes.

"You want him to hold you hand?" Holder asked.

Brewster swallowed hard. "Yeah. I do."

Holder nodded, giving Slocum a look that was supposed to be a smile, but looked more like a knife wound opening. His thin lips, just a little less pale than the ghostly pallor of his face, opened and closed in a fraction of a second.

Then, Holder slipped between two men and pushed open the door. He stepped aside and held it for Brewster. Slocum got there a few seconds later, and Holder nodded to him. "Evening," he said.

Slocum nodded back. "Evening."

When Slocum was on the porch, Holder followed him and let the door bang closed behind him. He reached into his pocket for a cigar, bit the end off it, and spat it out. Striking a match, he puffed loudly several times, turning the cigar to ignite the tip evenly. Satisfied, he cracked the match in two and tossed it into the darkness.

"You have a job for me, I understand," Holder said. His voice was surprisingly deep for a man so thin he looked almost frail. His hands, with their long, delicate-looking fingers, were heavily veined, and tendons stood out like cables in his wrists. There was real strength there, Slocum knew. Strength, and a total lack of concern for his own well-being.

"Yeah, I do," Brewster muttered.

"Tell me about it."

"What do you want to know?"

"Everything." Holder sat on the top step, his long

legs folding up toward his chest, and he rested his chin on his knees, puffing intermittently on the cigar.

"We've been having a bit of trouble, Mr. Holder."

"What sort of trouble?"

"There's been some rustling of cattle, and the big owners have decided that people like me and my friends are responsible for it. They're starting to put pressure on us."

"And you're sure none of your friends has been stealing cows?"

"Of course I'm sure. It's preposterous. Where would we put them? How could we hope to get away with it?"

"So you want me to do what, exactly?"

"We were sort of hoping you could lean on a few of them, get them to leave us alone."

"I don't lean on people, Brewster. You lean on them, they lean back. I kill people. You do that, they don't get to kill you back. Understand?"

"Well, I don't think it has to go that far."

"It always goes that far. It's already gone that far, or you wouldn't have come to me. Am I right?"

"Well, I . . ."

"You're right, Holder," Slocum said.

"How many dead, so far?"

"Three."

"Three nesters dead and . . ."

"No, not nesters. Cowhands. Two cowhands and a dentist."

"What?"

"That's right. Two cowhands. Both on the same ranch, the Westminster."

"One of them limey outfits, huh? Sounds like you already got somebody taking care of your dirty work, Brewster."

"No, we haven't. We haven't done anything of the kind."

"So you want me to find out who's been killing the cowboys, is that it?"

"No, we—we want to make sure that the cattlemen don't get out of control."

"They're out of control by their natures, Brewster. They only see things one way. They don't want anybody closing off the range, they don't want sheep cropping the grazing land down to the roots, and they sure as hell don't want anybody getting in the way of their cows. You people are in their way. You want them to forget about that, you're asking them to go against nature."

"And you're saying it doesn't happen, right?"

"That's right. I'm saying it doesn't happen."

"What can we do?"

"There's a couple or three things you could do. One is, you could all pack up and go on the hell back to St. Louis, or Philadelphia or Ohio, where you come from in the first place. You probably don't belong out here. People who do don't need people like me. Another thing you could do is cut some sort of a deal. Trouble with that is, most of the big ranchers don't know how to make a deal."

"And the third thing?"

"The third thing is you could send them a message."

"What sort of message?"

"Comes in a pine box. They usually understand it. If they do, it could be over just that easy. If they don't, well, then they send you a message back. And it goes on until one of you gets tired or until there's nobody left."

"We don't want a range war, Holder. We just want to be left alone."

"And you want me to hold your hand. I know all that. What I'm trying to tell you is it doesn't work like that. You want this thing finished, you let me handle it."

"How do you propose to do that?"

"I propose to do it without anybody looking over my shoulder. I promise results, Brewster. My methods are not your concern. Now, you know the price. Do we have a deal or did I waste my time riding all this way for nothing?"

Brewster looked at Slocum. "What do you think, Slocum? What should we do?"

"I think you're asking for trouble, Brewster. I think if you hire Mr. Holder, you can expect things to get a lot worse before they get better."

"You're partly right, cowboy," Holder said, tossing the cigar down and grinding it out under his heel. "They will get worse. Of course, they'll get worse either way. My way, though, they do get better. The other way, they don't."

"No, violence, right?" Brewster was almost pleading with the cadaverous gunman. "Right?"

"No unnecessary violence. Other than that, the only thing I guarantee is results."

"I don't know what to do. I . . ."

"You can talk to your friends and let me know in the morning. Or I can head on home. I get a fee for the consultation, either way. Just make up your mind."

"Do you mind if we talk alone for a minute?"

"Nope." Holder stood up and took another cigar from his jacket. He walked over toward Brewster's corral, where he propped a foot on the lowest rail and lit up.

"I think we should hire him, Slocum. I really do."

"I think it's a mistake, Brewster. The man's a hired killer. That's what he knows how to do. It's what he's good at. There's already been enough killing. And I'll tell you something else. Those cowhands, not just Stuart's, but all of them. They know how to use their guns. You people are babes in the woods. If it comes to a shooting war, there's no way you can win, Holder or no."

"I don't think that's necessarily so. Many of the small landowners are veterans. They've used guns. They've killed people."

"You don't understand how it works, Brewster. You work for an outfit like Stuart's, or any of the big ranches, you feel secure. You have friends you can count on. There's loyalty. Those men are used to working together. You people aren't. One of you gets the idea he'll be alright if he doesn't back you up, he might hesitate. He might even decide to sit on his hands. They can pressure you one by one. None of you will know whether you can count on help from anybody. But all those cowhands will know they can. They'll know somebody will watch their backs, somebody will help if they need it."

"Slocum, we're all in this together. I think we'll stick together. I think we'll help one another."

"Brewster, if you went inside now and put it to a vote, it would probably be unanimous. Not a man in that house thinks he'd run out on his neighbors. But half of them will, maybe more. You have not worked together under the gun. That takes time, that sort of trust and discipline."

"We don't *have* time, Slocum. Things are moving too fast."

"And what happens when Holder kills somebody? What do you do then?"

"It doesn't have to come to that. It won't."

"Yes, Linc, it will. You can count on it."

"It's the only chance we have, Slocum, don't you understand that?"

"Whatever you say."

"Will you stay and help us?"

"If Maggie asks me to, yes. Otherwise, no. I know what's coming, Brewster. And you'll wish to hell you never got started."

Brewster shook his head. "I hope you're wrong."

"So do I. But I'm not wrong."

Holder, sensing that their argument was drawing to a close, started back toward the porch. He placed one boot on the lowest step. "Well, what did you decide?"

Brewster stuck out a hand. "You've got a deal, Mr. Holder."

Holder grinned that thin-lipped grin again. He puffed on the cigar, and in the red tinged glow of it, he looked like nothing so much as a bloody skull.

16

"One thing's for damn sure, Slocum," Brewster said.

"Which is?"

"We got to organize some sort of patrols. Them cowboys are getting ready to wipe us out. We give them the chance, they'll level every small spread in this valley."

"Then why hire somebody like Holder? Why bring in a killer? It'll only lead to more killing."

"They started it."

"They think you started it. Hell, Brewster, it was Russ Higgins who was killed first. Then you and your friends jumped Luke Bradley. And Larry Holt was murdered in cold blood. You mean to tell me you didn't have anything to do with that?"

"As God is my witness."

"Then who did?"

"I don't know. But I'll tell you one thing, if I did know, I'd pin a medal on him. He done us a favor."

"Brewster, you're so damn blind with hatred, you can't even see what's happening. You're outnumbered, and you don't even have the law on your side. Ray Kandel is sympathetic, but Hardin was dead right. If Ray won't toe the mark, he'll be replaced."

"Maybe not, but even if we did, we still need some sort of organized protection. You don't know those people like I do, Slocum. They won't rest until every damn one of us is dead and buried. That's plain as the nose on your face. They mean to wipe us out and keep running their cattle where they damn please. But this land is ours, too. We got it fair and square. The Homestead Act didn't say we could stake a claim as long as we could hang onto it. It said if we staked a legal claim, the land was ours. No maybes, no unlesses. It's ours. And I mean to keep mine, Slocum. It's all I got. I put gallons of sweat in this damn earth. I cut them damn logs down with my own hands. I built this house. I mixed the goddamn mud smeared in the chinks. And Annie, my wife, God rest her soul, died right in that bedroom. You think I can walk away from all that, just because some damn cowman thinks the grass is his? Is that what you think?"

"No, of course not. But I think there's more going on here than you can explain. If you didn't kill Russ Higgins and Larry Holt, and Doc Wilson, then who the hell did?"

"Hell, I don't know. Maybe Higgins made an enemy somewhere along the line. Maybe it come back to haunt him."

"And Holt?"

"I don't know. That's a puzzlement, I admit. I knew Larry Holt, and I even kind of liked him. Doc Wilson, well that's a strange one, but, like you were saying, he was the one could put me in the clear on what happened to Higgins. Some cowboys knew that. Their bosses did too, most likely. But we run Luke Bradley off, and that's all we done. Anybody says different is a liar."

"Then I got a suggestion to make."

"Hell, Slocum, I'm all for settling this thing peaceably. You know that's true. But I just don't think it's possible. I truly don't. But if you got an idea, I sure as hell will do what I can. But don't ask me to send Holder packing. He's the only wall between us and them right now."

"Help me find out who penned those cows up in that ravine. Chances are, whoever was behind that killed Larry Holt. And maybe Russ too. Maybe he saw something when he went after them strays, something he wasn't supposed to see. Maybe the same man is behind all three of those events. I don't know for a fact, but it seems like it just might be possible."

"Alright. You let me take care of a few things, and I'll meet you any place you say. Four hours ought to be enough."

"Fine. I'll meet you at the ravine. That seems like as good a place as any to start looking."

"Hell, I don't know what you expect to find. Them two rustlers was killed wasn't anybody. Sheriff Kandel can't find anybody who knew who they were."

"You got a better idea, I'd love to hear it."

"You're doing this for Maggie Shaughnessy, ain't you?"

Slocum didn't answer.

"Hell, you don't have to say nothing. I know it's true."

"Four hours, at the ravine," Slocum said.

Against his better judgement, Slocum planned to visit the sheriff's office. He had a price on his head in half a dozen different jurisdictions. Wyoming wasn't one of them yet. But that luck might not hold much longer. Stuart and his cronies owned half the lawmen and most of the territorial politicians. If they put their minds to it, they could hog-tie him without doing much more than writing a half-dozen letters. Cheyenne was built with cattle money, and the territorial government knew it only too well.

On the plus side, Sheriff Kandel seemed like a decent man. He'd been fair to the settlers so far, but that might not last too much longer either. The way it usually worked was somebody put pressure on the lawman.

Choose up sides, he was told. You can keep your job if you side with us, and if you side with them, you can take your chances. It was not an easy choice, even for a man with a conscience.

Clearwater had a utilitarian approach to law enforcement. The sheriff, the mayor, and the circuit judge, who didn't come by often enough to suit either man, all shared space in the town hall. It had a jail, and it had a courtroom that doubled as a theater and tripled as a church on those rare Sunday mornings when a minister might happen through on his way to greener pastures. Nobody seemed to worry much about church and state, certainly not the mayor, and the sheriff didn't seem to think about the question at all.

Slocum tied his mount at the bleached and splintering hitching post out front, knocked on the glass-paneled door, and turned the knob. Kandel was at his desk, reading the monthly newspaper from Cheyenne. "Slocum," he said. "What can I do for you?"

"I was just talking to Linc Brewster. I was hoping you could give me a few minutes of your time."

"Hell, time's all I got. You want to borrow some, help yourself."

"You still haven't been able to identify those two dead rustlers, right?"

"Uh huh, that's right. What of it?"

"You been out to the ravine?"

"Nope. Once the bodies were brought in, it didn't seem like there was any reason to go out there at all. Why, you got an idea?"

"Not really. I just thought it might be a good place to start pulling on some loose threads. Maybe something will unravel."

"Most likely not. But you're welcome to tear the whole damn cloth apart, if it helps put the lid back on things. You tell Linc Brewster for me, next time you see him, this Holder is going to be more trouble than he's worth."

"I told him that already. But he's desperate, Sheriff,

they all are. They don't feel like they have a sporting chance. They think Stuart and the other big cattlemen have all the cards."

"Hell, Slocum, they do. You know that as well as I do. All the little man has is the law, and the law is for sale in Wyoming, even if the lawmen ain't. I come down on the wrong side, they just fire my ass and find somebody they like better."

"Where's that leave you?"

"In a tight corner, I guess. The floor's wet and the paint don't look like it'll dry anytime soon. You got a way out of that mess, you make sure I'm the first to know."

"I have a favor to ask."

"Can't lock a man up for that, Slocum."

"Can you put a hobble on Nate Holder?"

"You got a reason?"

"None you don't have."

"Hell, man, I can't lock up somebody because he might get into trouble. Don't have enough cells for that, and it ain't legal, anyhow."

"Maybe you could push him a little, make him step out of line."

"You looking to get my ass shot up, Slocum?"

"Just the reverse, actually. I'm hoping to see nobody gets shot."

"I wish I could help you, but that seems like it ain't fair. Tell you what I will do, though. I can watch him close, and if he steps out of line without pushing, maybe I can hold him a couple of days. Trouble is, he's got to cause big problems before I can do any more than that. I wish it was some other way, but it ain't."

"What about Doc Wilson? You learn anything?"

"Nope. Nothing's changed at all. Doc's still dead, and I still don't have a clue who killed him. Probably never will. That knife near the body looked like a good lead, but I came up empty."

"What about Clay Hardin."

"What about him?"

"He was in town just before the body was found. That was the same day he burned Maggie Shaughnessy's barn."

"That's true, and it's not something I overlooked. But nobody saw him anywhere near Doc's office. He didn't have a reason, so I guess unless he confesses, he's going to get away with it."

"But he did have a reason."

"What was that?"

"He claimed Linc Brewster was the one shot Russ Higgins. Only trouble with that was Linc says he was having a tooth pulled about the time Russ got shot."

"Hardin know about that?"

"I don't know for sure, but I think he might have."

"That's precious little to charge a man with murder, Slocum."

"I know, but it's more than you got on anybody else."

"Look, I'd like to help. I don't like watching them settlers get pushed around. But I can't lock up every man smells of cowshit, just to keep the peace."

Slocum nodded. "I understand. Thought it was worth a try, that's all."

"It was, but it just ain't enough. Look, Slocum, my daddy was a settler back in Kansas. We didn't have all these damn cows there then, but there was still some folks didn't like us. We come from New England, and feeling was running pretty high before the War. Hell, you should know about that. You must have heard about Quantrill, and what he did to Lawrence, back in the late fifties . . ."

"Sorry I bothered you, Sheriff."

"Look, get me something I can use, and I'm your man. But I need something real. Logic ain't enough, Slocum. I need cold, hard facts. And don't go sticking your nose in the beehive too deep, Slocum, or you'll get stung. Or worse . . ."

He felt no closer to a solution than when he arrived. Painful as it was to admit it, Kandel was right. All the way out to the ravine, he kept turning things over in his head. It was like looking at a giant puzzle with half the pieces missing. No matter which way he tried to put it together, he kept coming up against holes too big to ignore and impossible to work around.

He needed more pieces, and they were not going to fall in his lap. He had to go out and find them. Even then, it might not be enough. Holder was somewhere out there, too, and the longer it took Slocum to find what he needed, the more likely it was that someone who didn't have to was going to die.

By the time he reached the ravine, he was thoroughly discouraged. He still had nearly an hour before Brewster was due, and he pushed his horse up onto the rimrock. He hadn't been there since the shooting, and he tied up the chestnut and started to walk the edge.

Keeping his eyes on the ground, he scraped at every nook and cranny with the toes of his boots. There had to be something he could use, or at least something he could interpret, something that would at least point him in the right direction. For the time being, it didn't even matter whether it was something Kandel could use. The sheriff needed more than possibility. He needed certainty. But the possible was intriguing and could lead to the probable. Once he got his hooks into it, he just might be able to twist them enough to make something squeal.

17

Slocum was halfway around the rim, when he found it. Dropping to one knee, he examined the dry earth. The soil had been crushed under the agitated pace of nervous boot heels. Someone had been there for quite some time a few days before. As he pressed a patch of the earth, the dry crust broke, revealing moisture sealed in by the hard-baked top layer. But where the boots had been, the moisture was all gone. He stuck a finger into the ground all the way to the first knuckle. It came back bone dry.

That put it sometime after the last rainstorm, but long enough ago to have been the day Larry Holt was killed. Creeping to the edge, he looked down into the ravine and realized he had a clear shot at the place where Larry had been shot. That in itself was not surprising. What was surprising was the likelihood that someone had been waiting there for an hour or more. It wasn't possible any longer to write the episode off as a freak coincidence. Holt didn't just happen to have a run of bad luck. Someone had been waiting, knowing that Holt, or Slocum, or, for that matter, Clay Hardin was coming.

It was dry-gulching at its plainest and simplest. What was most enticing was the set of possibilities it excluded. Stuart wouldn't be stealing from himself. Larry Holt was not likely to commit suicide in so elaborate a way. Slocum had told no one. That limited the choices. Hardin was still on the list. But how many others? Who, if anyone, had Holt or Stuart told? What about the other stock growers who had been in Stuart's home that night? And as he thought about it, the list started to grow again. It just didn't work. There were too many possibilities. No matter how he tried to cut it, it came up useless.

Or almost.

The one indisputable fact was the constant presence of Clay Hardin. He had known about the ravine discovery. He had probably known Doc Wilson was Brewster's alibi. It was Hardin who had identified Brewster in the first place. Hardin had burned Maggie's barn. Under every rock, Clay Hardin, damp as a slug and just as ugly, turned up.

But why steal from his boss? What was the point? What was his motive? And who the hell was helping him?

Slocum kicked at the ground in frustration. He saw it too late, spiraling out and down, turning end over end, catching the sun and flinging it back at him in a series of blinding flashes. The cartridge casing landed far below and Slocum craned his neck to watch where it landed. It might be nothing, but small as it was, it was more than he had at the moment.

Slocum sprinted back to his horse and urged the surefooted animal back toward the mouth of the ravine. He started down the incline, looping to the right to reach the floor, when he spotted a lone rider far across the grassy valley, heading his way. Looking at his watch, he realized it must be Brewster. And off to the left, running parallel, a half mile back, three more riders.

They seemed to be matching him stride for stride, neither falling back nor closing the gap.

He couldn't tell whether Brewster knew they were there. Unless the farmer happened to look back, there was no way he could. He'd never hear their horses over the pounding hooves of his own. The slope was gentle, but gave Brewster a slight advantage at the half-mile lead. He could look back and down. But even if he knew they were there, there was no reason to suspect anything wrong.

But Slocum couldn't get rid of the tightness in his gut. It just seemed too much of a coincidence. The ravine was in the middle of nowhere. The only reason to come anywhere near it was the existence of the ravine itself. Or because someone else was headed there.

Thinking about the cartridge casing, he wondered if there might be a connection. Kandel had not been able to identify either of the gunmen who killed Larry Holt. Nor had they found the rifle of the man Holt had killed, the very man who had dropped the shell casing up on the rim. Was the rifle somehow significant? he wondered. Was that why they were following Brewster, afraid he might find it, and be able to throw some light on an otherwise dark corner of the plot?

For a moment, Slocum debated whether he should stay where he was or charge down to warn Brewster. He couldn't fire his gun, because that would alert the other riders and might only confuse Brewster. Still not certain what to do, he decided to stay where he was unless the pursuers started to close the gap.

There was a reasonable chance they didn't know Slocum was there, waiting for Brewster. If they thought to bushwhack him, Slocum might be able to learn something before throwing a shoe in the mill. Easing his horse in among some overgrown boulders, he tethered it to a sturdy shrub and unbooted his Winchester. He could no longer see Brewster or the riders, but he had no choice but to secrete himself and wait.

Brewster's horse soon drew within earshot. As it came closer, he could hear the big man's heavy breathing, the squeak of saddle leather. The horse had slowed, and Slocum strained to hear whether the followers were still charging headlong or if they, too, had slowed to a walk.

Brewster reached the trees and Slocum could hear the slow, tentative hooves of the horse pushing through the underbrush. Leaving his own mount, Slocum slipped among the trees down toward the gate. When he reached it, Brewster was standing there, one hand on the open gate, looking around.

"Brewster," he whispered. The big farmer spun around, nearly dropping his rifle in his surprise.

"Slocum, that you?"

"Over here," Slocum hissed. "Keep your voice down. We've got company."

Brewster looped his reins over the gate as Slocum moved into the open. "Come on, let's get under cover."

"What's going on?"

"I don't know. Three men followed you here. I was up top and spotted them right behind you. About a half mile or so."

"How do you know they were following me?"

"I don't, but I think we better assume the worst." He tugged Brewster into the trees, the big man stumbling as their feet struggled against the thick underbrush. He could hear the hooves now. The three men were whispering to one another, but they were too far away for him to make out the words.

Slocum tugged Brewster down among the rocks, then pointed toward the source of the muffled noise. "Let's see who it is," Slocum whispered. "Don't shoot unless they shoot first."

"I think we should hit them first."

"No, it's more important to find out what the hell is going on."

Slocum kept a grip on Brewster's arm, yanking him back when the big farmer tried to move away. "Stay here, damn it."

A moment later, the three riders broke through the first line of trees. From his vantage point, Slocum was looking down on them. None of the men was familiar.

Bringing his lips close to Brewster's ear, he asked, "You ever seen any of them before?"

Brewster shook his head.

The tallest of the three seemed to be the leader. He turned to the other two. "I told you bastards we shouldn't have waited. You're too damned greedy, didn't I tell you? Now we got nothing."

"How the hell should we have known somebody would find them steers?"

"You didn't have to know. There's just such a thing as pushing your luck. I kept telling you, take it smaller, go more often. Twenty-five thousand dollars, gone like that." He snapped his fingers, and the crack snapped like breaking wood in the hot afternoon.

"What are we doing here? Stuart got all the cattle back. What's the point?"

"Where the hell's Brewster?"

"What difference does it make?"

"We didn't come all the way out here for me to answer a damn fool question like that, Max. Now did we? Because if we did, maybe I need to find some new partners. You're too stupid to blow your own nose."

"No need for that, Trask. You know what I mean."

"We come out here to put Brewster away. That's why we come out here. And if we can make it look like he's behind the rustling, so much the better. We got to walk a tight line here. Playing both ends against the middle ain't as easy as it sounds."

"What difference does it make? Them cows are long gone."

"But it worked, Max. It worked, didn't it? And if it worked once, it'll work again. I told you my man had a great idea."

"It takes too damn long."

"You got a better idea?"

"No . . ."

"Then shut up. Let's find that fat bastard and do what we come to."

They broke up their whispered conference and the man called Trask headed for the gate. A moment later he called to the others. "Here's his horse. He can't be far."

"Probably listening to us right now."

"Three against one, he can listen all he wants. That's about as far as it goes."

"The gate's open, he must have gone in."

Slocum started to move.

"Where you going?" Brewster whispered.

"I want to stay with them. You stay here. Once you're sure they're well inside, get their horses out of the way. Move them fifty or sixty yards, just enough so they can't get to them in a hurry."

"And what are you going to do?"

"I want to stay close. So far we don't know any more than we did before they got here. If they keep talking, maybe we'll learn something. I want to know who the 'man' they're talking about happens to be."

"Slocum, you be careful in there."

Slocum grinned. "I didn't live this long being careless, Linc."

The three men were moving cautiously, keeping to cover and stopping to listen every ten or fifteen yards. Slocum moved when they moved, trying to keep them in sight. They had fallen silent, and he was too far to hear anything but a shout in any case.

The ravine floor showed all the signs of the herd. Piles of manure were everywhere, and the grass was chewed down almost to its roots. Even some of the brush showed signs of hungry gnawing. The longhorns ate almost anything when food was scarce. Still, it was clear that the cattle must have been moved out to graze at night. There just wasn't enough food for that many steers in the narrow canyon.

The deeper they went, the more relaxed the men seemed. They spread out a little, leaving twenty or thirty feet between them. They advanced singly now, two stay-

THE WYOMING CATTLE WAR 121

ing back to cover while one moved ahead to the next cover. Halfway in, one of the men pointed to the rim, and Slocum followed the finger. At first he was puzzled. He saw nothing up top, then realized the man had pointed to the lair of Holt's killer.

The men angled in toward the wall now. They moved ahead without concern for cover. As they reached the base of the wall, a shot rang out. Slocum snapped his head to the right. A second shot, then a third, cracked, the report bouncing from wall to wall and back. One of the men fell to the ground. The other two dove. Slocum looked at the rim behind them. He couldn't see a thing, but the men were convinced they had been fired on from up above.

Another shot exploded, and Slocum heard a groan from one of the men. So far, the sniper seemed not to know anyone else was in the ravine. Sporadic return fire cracked from the base of the wall, and puffs of dust exploded high on the rim. Chips of red rock started to cascade down into the ravine, knocking others loose and showering the treetops against the far wall.

Slocum kept his eye on the rim, but the shooter, and there seemed to be only one, was too well concealed. He fired again and again, and this time no one fired back.

He moved quietly, keeping as much brush as he could between him and the sniper. Angling in toward the near wall, he dropped to his belly and slithered under the brush until he was close enough to see where the three rustlers had taken cover. One man was clearly dead. He lay on his stomach, a huge bloody stain on the back of his shirt glistening in the sunlight filtering down through the treetops. His gun lay just ahead of his outstretched fingers.

A sudden shower of rock spewed over the rim, and a moment later, he heard hoofbeats, gradually growing softer as the sniper made his getaway. Slocum crawled closer, listening for the slightest sound. The ravine was deathly still.

"Hello," Slocum called. "Anyone there?"

His voice echoed, then died. It could be a trap, and he had to be careful, but something told him the sniper had done his work well. Sliding in among loose rocks, he covered his head with his hands when several fist-sized chunks of red rock crashed down around him. They landed on a pile of scree and skidded to the bottom. Sand sifted through the air with the noise of insects, then it, too, stopped.

Slocum found the second rustler leaning against the wall. A bullet had slammed into his forehead and splattered his brains against the rock behind him. His eyes were still open, and they seemed to be watching Slocum with infinite patience, never blinking, never shifting their gaze for a second. Slocum suppressed a shiver and crawled closer. Reaching the rocks, he waited for a long moment, watching the rim for any sign of life.

Convinced there was no one there, he crept around a huge slab of red rock leaning over against a rounded boulder. The third man huddled behind the rocks. Slocum thought he saw a movement, and ducked. Watching in silence, it dawned on him that the man was not breathing. He dashed across a small open space and ducked in behind the red slab.

The third gunman had crouched down too late. A bullet had ripped through his shoulder and, from the looks of things, broken several bones before exiting. The pool of blood on the ground was all the evidence Slocum needed.

Three men had followed Linc Brewster.

All three were dead.

Someone had known, and that someone was still out there.

18

"It's never going to end, is it?" Maggie said. She walked to the window and pulled the curtain aside to look out at the night. In the soft light from the single lantern, her face was hidden in shadows. "It seems like it's been going on forever."

She let the curtain drop and walked to the door. Slocum thought for a moment she was going to lock up for the night. Instead, she pushed out onto the porch, letting the screen bump softly closed behind her.

"Slocum, come on outside. It's a beautiful night."

He pushed his chair back and walked to the door. Maggie was standing just off the porch, and his shadow spilled out over the front steps and down. Maggie's hand idly stroked a thigh, just where the silhouette of his head rested above her knee.

He opened the screen and walked to the steps, taking a seat on the rough wood while Maggie walked in small circles, a single straw in her hand fanning the air. "It's so pretty, it's almost impossible to believe that anyone died today. Needlessly, so needlessly."

"It won't be the last, Maggie. I think it's about time you told me everything."

"What do you mean?"

"I mean how all this started. I know there's more to it than anybody's letting on."

"You're too suspicious, John Slocum. Too suspicious by half."

"Maybe. But I think there's something between the Stuarts and the Shaughnessys that no one is telling me. Everybody seems to take it for granted. But I don't know what it is."

"Why do you say that?"

"Just something I sensed when Mary Alice gave me the money for your barn. It was the way she did it, and the way you reacted when I told you about it."

"Old wounds, Slocum. Sometimes they stop bleeding, but they never heal. It's like that."

"What happened?"

"It won't change anything if you know."

"It might."

"It won't help me to talk about it."

"How do you know, unless you try?"

"Don't push it, please, John. Just don't."

She started walking away from the house. Slow steps, but it was clear she was trying to run away from something. She turned the corner of the house, and Slocum got up to go after her. When he turned the corner, she broke into a run, down behind the house and to the fence. She placed one foot on the lowest split rail and vaulted over easily, landing on her feet and breaking into a sprint.

"Maggie, wait!" Slocum called. He took the fence at full speed, barely breaking stride as he raced into the grass. There was a bright moon, and its light washed over the grass, turning the gray-green to a matte silver. Maggie looked like something carved out of pure night against the gray-white meadow.

"Come back!" Slocum shouted. But she ignored him,

heading downhill toward a small brook lined with trees. It was two hundred yards or more, and Maggie was halfway there already. Her silhouette got lost among the skeletons of trees, and Slocum followed the bent grass when he lost sight of her.

He could hear her heavy steps, even her breathless panting, but she kept on running, as if something terrible were following her, or something too real and too painful to confront.

He hated pushing her like that, but if he was going to put his head on the block, he had to know everything. She was the key, somehow, and even Maggie seemed to know it. Panting, his knees aching from the constant pounding, he reached the trees. Stopping to listen, he realized that Maggie had stopped as well.

"Maggie?" he called. "Maggie, where are you?"

"Leave me alone," she shouted. Her voice bounced back to him from the wall of the new barn, then dropped dead in the long grass.

"Come on, Maggie, where are you?"

This time, she didn't answer. He took a half-dozen steps toward the sound of her voice, hoping to spook her. If she started to run, he could track her. But if she stayed calm, he could hunt for hours without finding her. Taking care to muffle his steps, he moved another ten feet. A shadow passed across the face of the moon, and the light dimmed considerably. Glancing up through the dark trees, he saw the brilliant white edge of the huge cloud, its dark heart blacker than the sky behind it.

"Maggie?" This time she bolted, and he was closer than he realized. She splashed across the brook, and he darted through the brush down to the water's edge. He tried jumping across. Slippery moss underfoot sent him skidding and he fell backward, landing heavily in the water with a huge splash.

He cursed in exasperation. "That's no language, John Slocum. You're making me ears burn."

"More than that will burn, if I get my hands on you, Maggie Shaughnessy. I'm serious now. You have to talk to me." He hauled himself to his feet, carefully placed a foot on the same slippery rock, and fell again. With a sigh, he fell backward, letting the icy water wash over him.

Slocum surfaced, took a deep breath, and plunged back into the water. He lay still, ignoring the chill. Maggie's voice came to him from a great distance. "Slocum? Are you alright, John? Answer me."

He let a few bubbles escape. His lungs were starting to protest when he felt her hands grab him just below the knees. She started to pull, and he jackknifed up out of the water, letting his breath explode, and filled his lungs with cool, fresh air. He snagged her wrists and pulled.

She tried to jerk free, but lost her footing on the bank and toppled toward him. He started back, breaking her fall with his body, and she struggled like a hooked trout.

"Oh, you bastard," she shouted. "John Slocum, you're a devil."

She was as soaked as he was now. She stopped struggling and rolled over, letting the water soak those few stray islands of her still somehow dry. Spluttering and laughing, she sat up, then sliced a palm across the water, sending a great sheet of spray into his face.

He splashed back, and for more than a minute, neither of them was more than ten years old. Slicing and slapping at the water, they doused one another repeatedly. Maggie's hair sagged with the heavy weight of the water, and she stopped splashing long enough to pull the pins and shake it free. It fell past her shoulders, its brilliant red a dark, muddy brown between the water and the indifferent light.

"You've gone and near drowned me, John Slocum. And I thought you were hurt, lying there like a dead fish. You shouldn't scare me like that. I have a weak heart."

"Do you, now?"

"Aye, I do."

He reached out to touch her cheek, and she buried her chin in her chest. Gently, he tilted her head back, grinning at the havoc the water had wrought. "You look beautiful," he said.

"And if I do, you look like Saint Patrick himself."

He let his hand fall away, but she caught it and brought it back to her lips. "You make me feel the fool, John Slocum."

He leaned forward and kissed her full on the mouth. At first, she froze. Her lips clamped down tight for a moment, then opened wide and her tongue slid into his mouth. He responded, and she locked her arms around him, pinning his own arms to his sides.

As suddenly as it started, she let him go. She stood up and backed away from him. The cloud overhead finally slid past the moon, and the silver light returned. He could see her clearly for the first time, as her hands worried with the buttons of her woolen shirt. She continued to back away from him, tripped on the grassy bank, and sat down heavily.

Maggie opened her shirt and pulled it off as Slocum walked toward her on his knees. Still in the water, he ignored the cold current swirling around him and felt himself begin to stiffen, even in the cold.

She lay back on the grass and started on the buttons of her dungarees. Arching her hips just as he reached her, she tugged the pants partway down. He grabbed the water-thickened denim and pulled them all the way down. Her boots came away with the dungarees, and he tossed the sodden clothes up behind her into the shadows.

Kneeling between her thighs, he leaned forward and traced the curve of a thigh with the tip of his tongue. She shivered, and he knew it had nothing to do with the cold. The pebbled skin, so smooth in spite of the chill, damp with the brook water, slid beneath his tongue like a piece of silk. At her bush, he flicked away several sparkling drops of water shimmering in the thick red curls, then traced the inner curve of the other thigh.

"Don't you be a tease, now, John Slocum," she whispered. He started back up her leg, this time diving to the bottom edge of the auburn thatch and slid the tip of his tongue between thick, musky lips. The taste of her was salty, tangy, and he twirled his tongue in the juicy flesh, sliding it in as far as he could. He slipped his hands under her, lifted her toward him a bit, and lapped at her eagerly. The scent of her made him giddy. Every stroke of his tongue, its hiss on her flesh, the burbling wetness of her, made him hungrier.

She reached down for him, taking him roughly by the hair and pulling him higher. He licked his way up between her breasts and took one stiff nipple between his teeth. She kept wriggling, and he pressed a damp knee against her, massaging her as he sucked at one breast, then the other.

Maggie pulled him higher still, pressing him down against her body as if she wanted to absorb him totally. With one hand, she clawed at his belt and buttons, then tugged furiously at his dungarees. He felt himself suddenly free of the confining cloth and her hand curled around his erection and began to stroke him. She breathed in short, sharp gasps, hot and wet in his ear, panting as she stroked him faster and faster.

Then, so suddenly it caught him off balance, she spread her legs wide and bucked her hips. Her hand guided him in and he drove home with a single thrust, piercing her so deeply she gasped in surprise.

The gasp turned to a moan, and she squeezed him harder, working her hips slowly back, then forward. He found her rhythm and probed deeply with each thrust. Her fingers dug deeply into his flesh, urging him to go still deeper. Her hips cracked against his with the sound of bone on bone, and he breathed faster and faster, matching her gasp for gasp. Another moan, this one from somewhere deep in her chest, became an animal cry and she whipped her legs around him, holding him fast.

"Don't move," she whispered, almost crushing him between her thighs. Her hand fluttered on the cold skin of his back, sliding up under his shirt and stroking him gently. "Don't move."

Slowly, he could feel the tension drain out of her. She

relaxed as if she were melting wax, then let him slip out of her with a damp sucking sound. Still hard, he crawled alongside her and lay on his back. Her fingers found him and gently stroked him, keeping him hard, her juices bubbling under her caressing fingers.

"Now, what did you want to know?" she whispered.

"Everything," he said.

She continued to stroke him, responding to his questions with a squeeze when one hit home. But she told him everything, just as he asked.

When she stopped talking and he said nothing, she asked, "Is there anything else you want to know?"

"No," he whispered.

She started to stroke him faster, her fingers kneading the rock-hard length of him. "I think I need this now," she said, squeezing even harder.

Slocum lifted her, and she spread her legs as he lowered her down, the chill of the cold night air vanishing as she enveloped him.

"Yes," she whispered. "I do need it so."

19

The sun on his face woke Slocum a little after five-thirty. He sat up still dazed from the previous night. He looked for Maggie, but she was already up. He dressed quickly and walked into the kitchen. The front door was open, and he walked out onto the porch. The sun, even at the early hour, felt hot on his skin. He looked down at his hands, stained orange by the light.

Maggie was at the well, working the handle slowly to top off the wooden pail. He stepped off the porch. "Let me get that for you," he said.

"I can manage." She smiled. He joined her at the pump and looked up at the cloudless sky. It finally cleared the horizon, and its color began to fade to yellow, and then to white. In a few minutes, it had gone from bloodred to almost no color at all. The sky was deeper blue than normal.

Maggie saw him looking at the sky. "It's going to be a hot one," she said.

"I can't wait until fall."

"That's my favorite . . ."

"Sssshhh," he hissed. "Listen . . ."

Out on the plains, they heard hoofbeats. A single horse was running at top speed, drawing closer with every stride. The rider urged the animal on with high-pitched shouts, and when he broke over the ridge, they could see him lashing frantically with the loose end of the reins.

"That's Clay Hardin," Slocum said, sprinting for the house.

"Where are you going?"

"To get my gun."

Maggie rushed after him. "I don't want any shooting, not with Brian here. Please, John, what I told you last night, that was between us. I'm trying to bury that part of my life."

"You can't bury something like that, Maggie. Besides, that has nothing to do with it. Hardin has been after me since the beginning. If he catches me unarmed, I can kiss my ass good-bye."

He leapt to the porch and ran to the bedroom. Grabbing the gun belt, he spun back through the door, whipping it around his hips and buckling the gun belt in a single, fluid motion. Brian heard the commotion and peeked out of his room.

"What's happening?" he asked.

"Nothing. Just stay inside, Brian. Whatever you do, don't come out."

Hardin nearly fell from his mount as the horse stormed into the lane at full gallop. The horse started to shy away as it approached the house. Slocum was on the porch, the Colt Navy in his hand. Hardin, if he noticed the gun, was not intimidated. He jumped from the saddle and charged straight up onto the porch.

"You bastard," he shouted, "where is she?"

He lunged at Slocum, trying to grab him by the throat. Slocum ducked under the grasping hands and landed a jab into Hardin's midsection. The foreman staggered back a step and doubled over. He lost his footing on the edge of the porch and slipped to the ground, slamming one knee into the sharp edge of the raw timber.

Ignoring the pain, Hardin scrambled to his feet. "Where is she?" he shrieked again.

"Where is who?" Slocum demanded. Maggie cocked the hammers on a double-barreled shotgun, and Hardin whirled when he heard the metallic click.

"Mary Alice," he said. "What have you done with her?"

"I haven't done anything with her. I don't know what you're talking about. Hardin, make sense, man."

"You took her, you bastard. I know you did."

"I didn't take anybody."

"You're lying, Slocum. I ought to gut you right now."

"Hardin, why don't you slow up and try to make some sense. What happened?"

"Don't play dumb with me, Slocum. I swear it, I'll kill you yet."

"Hardin, I swear to you, I don't have the faintest idea what you're talking about."

"She's gone. She didn't come to dinner last night. She wasn't in her room this morning. It had to be you. She wouldn't run off like that. It had to be you."

"No."

He turned to Maggie. "Make him tell me where she is."

"You have the nerve to ask for my help, after what you did to my brother!"

Hardin staggered as if she had punched him. He sat down hard on the porch.

"I ought to blow you to pieces, Clay Hardin. And don't think I won't. Just give me an excuse."

Hardin stared at her, his eyes bulging. His lips moved like those of a gasping fish, but nothing but a croak came out of his mouth. "Don't," he managed to say. "Please, don't..."

Maggie advanced on him, the shotgun held in front of her like a jouster's lance. Hardin squirmed in his place, then tried to crawl backward onto the porch. "Stay right there," Maggie snarled. She stabbed at him with the twin muzzles of the Remington. Hardin winced as if she'd struck him, and she took another step forward.

Poking him in the chest with the shotgun, she allowed the muzzles to rest against his breastbone. "Now, give me one reason I shouldn't kill you."

"I—I..." he stammered, "I... don't, please..."

Brian appeared in the front doorway. "Mom, what's going on? What's happened?"

"Brian, go back inside. Now!"

"But..."

"John, take him inside, please."

Slocum opened the screen door and put a hand on Brian's shoulder. Keeping his eyes fixed on Hardin, he said. "Brian, everything's alright. Go on inside. Your mom's just upset."

"She's not going to shoot him, is she?"

"The hell I'm not," Maggie snapped. She glared at him then, as if she suddenly realized what she was doing, she shook her head. "No, son, I'm not going to shoot anybody."

Hardin sighed and started to relax, but Maggie prodded him sharply with the gun barrels. "Mr. Slocum did not take the girl. That's your speed, not his. He does not know where she is. And if you *ever* come back here, by God, I *will* kill you. Don't think I won't. Now, get on your horse and get off my land."

Getting nervously to his feet, Hardin moved toward the edge of the porch as Maggie backed away.

"Hold it, Hardin."

Hardin turned around, as if confronted by another threat. Slocum waved the barrel of the Colt. "Leave your gun."

"But..."

"Leave it or get buried with it. Your choice."

Taking Slocum's cue, Maggie walked toward Slocum's horse and yanked his rifle out of the boot.

"You're not going to send me out there unarmed, are you? With everything that's been going on?"

"The hell I'm not," Slocum snapped. "If you think I want you to turn around and back shoot me before I get through the door, you're mistaken."

"I wouldn't do that. I . . ."

"Yes," Maggie shouted, "you would. You did. You murdered my brother. I can't prove it, but I know it. And if ever I *can* prove it, you won't have to worry about standing trial, Clay Hardin. I'll kill you myself, no matter what it takes."

Hardin backed away from her and reached for the reins. He swung into the saddle like a novice, nearly losing his balance and falling off the other side. "You haven't heard the last of this, Slocum. And if you hurt Mary Alice . . ."

"What? You'll what? Ambush me the way you did Pat Hennegan?"

Slocum unholstered Hardin's Peacemaker and pointed it toward the sky. He squeezed the trigger and Hardin lashed at his mount. Slowly, Slocum fired again and again, until the revolver was empty. When Hardin was little more than a silhouette against the skyline, Slocum finally sighed.

"I think I better talk to Addison Stuart," he said.

"You can't. You wouldn't stand a chance over there."

"I'll be alright. As long as they think I've taken the girl, they won't dare kill me."

"But what's the point?"

"Whatever is wrong with her father, she doesn't deserve this. She's a decent kid. And you, Brewster, and the others will be blamed for it if anything does happen to her."

"But what can you do?"

"I don't know. But I think I know who did kidnap her."

"How could you know that?"

"I think it was Nate Holder."

"I told Brewster not to hire that man, but he wouldn't listen to me."

"Too late for that, now."

"What are you going to do?"

"I'll need some help. If Stuart understands what's going on, he just might be willing to cooperate."

"Why not use Linc?"

"You people can't afford to leave yourselves unprotected. Even if Stuart thinks I'm holding his daughter, he won't try anything for fear of her being harmed. But I'm not so sure about the others. They talk cooperation, but I think they're all in it for themselves. One man's meat. You know the saying. Besides, if I can siphon off some of the hands, there'll be that much less likelihood of an attack against you all."

"What do you want me to do?"

"I want you to get hold of Linc Brewster and tell him what's happened. I'll get back to you as soon as I can. But not until I know what's going on."

Slocum saddled his horse and Maggie stood beside him, wringing her hands. "Suppose something happens to you, John."

Slocum shook his head. "Nothing's going to happen."

"But suppose..."

"Maggie, you took care of yourself fine before I came along. You can do it after I'm gone."

"Don't talk like that."

Slocum climbed into the saddle, and Maggie followed him halfway down the lane. "Be careful. Please, be careful."

Slocum waved without looking back. He was afraid that if he did, he might not have the courage to go. Despite what he told her, there was at least a fifty-fifty chance that Stuart might try to detain him or, worse yet, kill him on sight. But that was a chance he'd have to take. He couldn't shake the feeling that his life wasn't the only one hanging in the balance.

So many lives were so tightly bound together, over land that belonged to none of them and cows that didn't know they even existed. It all seemed so foolish. There was no need for any of it, but events had left logic far behind. They had a momentum of their own, now, like a freight train running downhill, and Nate Holder was back there somewhere, his shoulder to the caboose, giving it an extra push.

The Stuart spread seemed deserted as he rode through the gate. It was possible the men were all out already, looking for the missing girl. Slocum made sure his revolver was loose, and climbed the steps. Whitcomb met him on the porch.

"I'm surprised to see you, sir."

"I'll bet you are. Mr. Stuart around?"

"In the study, sir."

"I know the way."

Slocum found the dour Scotsman slumped in a high-backed chair behind his desk. He looked up with glazed eyes when Slocum entered.

Stuart didn't seem surprised to see him. He nodded, then tossed a sheet of paper across the desk. It landed at Slocum's feet. He bent to retrieve it, keeping his eyes on Stuart. When he snatched the paper off the carpet, he unfolded it with one hand, then smoothed it against his thigh.

He read it twice through, before saying anything.

"Good speller, isn't he?"

"You noticed, did you."

"I'm not a barbarian, Mr. Stuart."

"But you are a bit of a fool, coming here like this."

"You know I had nothing to do with this."

"Do I?"

"Of course you do."

Stuart stared at the ceiling, his eyes half-closed. "'If you want to see the girl again, call off your dogs. John Slocum.' I've read it a thousand times, Slocum. I know every word by heart."

"I didn't send it."

"Then why are you here?"

"Because I want to see this ended. Not just Mary Alice returned unharmed, but all of it. You have a lot of influence around here, Mr. Stuart. And you're a stubborn son of a bitch. But I think you know time and history are against you. Maybe the others don't, but you do. And you can help make sure no one else gets hurt."

"That sounds like the same philosophy as the note."

"Maybe so. But..."

"What do you want me to do?" Stuart looked at Slocum hard, his eyes bright, almost glittering in the light sifting through the lace curtains. "I'll do anything you want. Just bring my daughter back safe, Slocum."

20

Finding Nate Holder was like finding a needle moving from haystack to haystack. The gunman was shrewd, and he had the advantage of the offensive. But kidnapping Mary Alice Stuart could be a liability, and Slocum had to find a way to use it to his advantage. If Holder had taken the girl, he had two choices—either he could drag her from place to place, substantially hindering mobility, or he could keep her a prisoner in some secure place. But if he took the latter tack, his range would be limited. He would have to return to her prison every day or so, to make sure she had enough to eat and drink, and to make certain she was still there.

Either choice presumed Holder was working on his own. If he had help, all bets were off. Holder could come and go as he pleased, without the kidnapped girl hampering him in the least.

Trying to figure kept Slocum running in circles. He didn't know anything about Nate Holder personally. But the type was anything but novel. Slocum had known a dozen men just like him. And none of those men worked with a partner. Suspicious by nature, made more so by the nature of their occupations, they wished to be as free of encumbrance as possible, and that meant free of assistants. Holder had to be cut from the same cloth.

Which brought Slocum back to his first two options. Holder's suspicions wouldn't be likely to make him happy with the notion of his trump card spending her days unattended. But playing hit and run was a tough enough row to hoe with a millstone in petticoats strung around his neck.

It wasn't too likely that Holder would just sit on his hands. He was too restless for that, and too sure of himself. He would want to rub Stuart's nose in the dirt, make an issue of Stuart's helplessness. The mighty rancher, with dozens of men in his employ, and half a dozen friends with several dozen more to do their bidding, and they were powerless to stop a single man from wreaking havoc on their way of life. That is how Holder would see it.

Mary Alice was his shield. As long she remained under his control, they wouldn't dare kill him. He could sit on the perimeter and harass them at will, even kill a few of them, as long as they weren't heavyweights. Mary Alice was the daughter of one of the most influential men in the Clearwater basin. Alive, she was useful to Nate Holder, dead she was worse than worthless, she would be the cause that would bring him down.

Since he had no idea where Holder might be, there was only one way to find him, and that was to watch his potential targets. Holder was almost certain to ratchet the pressure a notch or two at a time. For the time being, Stuart himself was safe. You don't take a man's daughter and hold her for ransom if you plan to shoot the man. It was an extra step and a risky one. The same would be true of the other big cattlemen. They were businessmen, and that meant they knew how to make deals.

Deals meant an exchange. Nate Holder was going to

start charging them. Most likely the currency would be blood. It was the thing men like Holder understood best. Slocum headed out to the open range. With the roundup coming on in earnest, there would be crews all over the high country, rounding up the cattle, shipping off their own, and passing the others along to work crews from the other outfits.

Slocum could wait on Holder to make his move, then follow him to wherever he had holed up with Mary Alice. Six miles from Clearwater, he came on the first team, pushing a few hundred head of Stuart beeves down toward the branding corral. With the summer drawing to a close, it was almost time to drive a herd to Fort Kearney for winter meat. The crews were skittish now, and Slocum didn't blame them. As like as not, they would shoot him before bothering to find out who he was. That made the open range a dangerous place for a solitary rider, but there was no other way to go.

He picked a slope-shouldered butte as his watchtower. From the high, flat-topped slab, he could see for miles in every direction. Pushing his horse up the switchbacks on the wedge end of the butte, he climbed higher and higher in the endless blue sky. Once he reached the top, the horse panting, even staggering a little, Slocum dismounted. He grabbed his binoculars and moved cautiously to the western edge of the huge block of red rock. Although its profile seemed almost perfectly straight across the horizon when viewed from the valley floor, the reality was much less ideal.

Littered with broken rock, its surface less like a table than that of a thick blanket snapped open but not smoothed out, the butte was half a mile long and almost the same width. Even without his glasses, he could see wispy columns of smoke from the branding fires. Temporary corrals, their rails like toothpicks at this range, seemed full of bubbling brown fluid. Only through the glasses could he make out the individual steers. Picking the southernmost fire, he twiddled the focus enough to zero in on two men bent over the flames. Neither one looked familiar. It was not a Westminster crew.

The second fire was a dry hole as well. Scarecrow and a couple of the others, Luke Bradley among them, were cutting young steers from a new herd. With every calf roped and branded, Slocum thought he could smell the stench of burnt hair, the sickly sweet tang of seared hide. He could hear the hiss of the iron as it stamped the Stuart brand on a trembling flank. Then, back into the fire with bits of hair still curled and clinging to the metal, the iron was reheated and Scarecrow grabbed a new one for the next calf, and the next.

Tedious, backbreaking work to the tune of a dollar a day, it seemed as if the supply of calves was endless. Like some scene from cowboy hell, the steers kept coming, teams of three and four and five, driving cattle in bunches from dozens to a hundred. Beige clouds gathered in the air over the corrals, dust that had lain for months, even years, suddenly kicked into the sky, boiling and eddying with every change in the wind.

The fires were spread out to give the outfits working room. Nobody wanted to get in anybody's way, but nobody wanted to move any farther than he had to. Certainly not in service of an endless stream of cattle. It sometimes seemed two calves were born with every sizzling brand burned home, as if the process spawned itself, and then kept itself alive and fed by generating work faster than it could be done.

Slocum covered a dozen fires from the north to the south. Behind him, separated from the other work crews by the massiveness of the butte, a couple more small groups performed their own version. But there was so little variation, it wasn't possible to tell one from another. Even with the glasses, the brand itself was little more than a black smear in a cow's hide. What brand, and who the owner was, were things that mattered only at close range. At this distance, they might as well have been prodding the cattle with white-hot sticks. Leave a dark scar behind, any scar you please. It was little enough compensation for an otherwise thankless job.

Slocum was about to swing back to the western side of the butte. He glanced over his shoulder and watched his horse for a few moments, then got to his feet. He was already moving when he heard it, the big, booming thunderclap of a buffalo gun. The slug could travel for a mile or more and, in the hands of an expert, could kill not only the buffalo himself but a specific fly settling on the thick, hairy hide.

The buffalo were all but gone in this part of the country, but the hunters were still out there.

Or were they?

He heard the second shot, rolling up like the gathering roar of an avalanche gaining speed. It slapped the rocks behind him, turning brittle before rebounding and rushing past him again. Training the glasses on one work team after another, he saw no sign that would tell him who, if anyone, was under attack. Several men stood to listen, their heads cocked, their hats tipped back or even held in their hands.

He was watching Scarecrow's team when Luke Bradley flew from his saddle. At first, Slocum thought the cowhand had dismounted in a hurry, but the sound of the third shot drifting lazily skyward changed his mind. At that distance the difference in velocity between the bullet and the sound of the rifle was disconcerting. He'd seen the effect of the shot before he knew it had been fired.

Scarecrow, so tiny in the glasses, rushed to Bradley and knelt down. Then the tall man looked up at the sky, scanning the horizon for some sign. When he spun to look at the butte, Slocum could read the terror in his face.

Convinced now that someone was sniping long range at Stuart's men, Slocum felt helpless. The buffalo gun had a range of better than a mile. The shooter could be anyplace. There was only one way to find him. Inscribing a one-mile circle with the glasses, he looked for the telltale traces of gunsmoke, some small cloud hanging in the air where it didn't belong.

Yard by yard, he covered the ground, looking for the slightest trace. So far nothing. He covered the perimeter a second time, one fist squeezing the glasses, the other clenched in frustration.

Then he got lucky. A spurt, almost like steam, at least a yard long, speared toward Bradley and Scarecrow's branding fire. Dying to know what effect the shot had, Slocum gritted his teeth, refusing to look. The sound smacked him, so loud he could almost feel it, this time. The smoky finger began to expand, then to break into wispy tatters.

A clump of jack pines, just inside the one-mile mark, was the sniper's lair. Slocum trained the glasses on the trees, but he could see nothing, no movement, no flash of light, nothing but the torn rags of smoke already beginning to dissipate. He raced to his horse and sprang into the saddle, reaching behind to stuff the glasses into an open saddlebag even as the horse started to move.

He pushed the animal against its natural caution. Driving it through a rocky defile taller than his head, he wondered if the shooter was Nate Holder. But he didn't wonder long. It had to be.

Making his way down the slope of the butte, he had to circle away from the gunman. Listening with one ear all the way down, he didn't hear any more gunfire. At the bottom, he had a difficult choice to make. On horseback, he would be a sitting duck. On foot, he might never get to Holder before the gunman either changed positions or broke off the attack altogether. Slocum opted for a middle course. He rode in a shallow loop, trying to get behind Holder without letting on he knew where the gunman lay hidden.

Keeping the clump of pines on his left, he forded a shallow stream, screening himself with the dense brush growing along the water's edge. Slocum kept waiting for the next clap of thunder. His whole body was tight, his shoulders drawn in, his fists clenched. He could hear his teeth scraping and grinding against one another as he worked his jaw.

A half mile farther on, he dropped from the saddle and crept through the brush, the glasses draped around his neck. He could see the jack pines, their dark bark and skinny trunks like a fistful of black fingers. Again he waited for some telltale sign. Anything, a flash of light on polished metal, smoke from a cigarette, anything at all to tell him Holder was still there. But the pines stood silent, swaying slightly in the breeze.

It was more than a quarter mile to the stand of trees, with nothing to cover his approach but some tall grass and a few boulders. He started to step into the water when something caught his eye. Quickly, he swung the glasses up, cursing as he tried to find the trees.

He saw it again, a slight movement, then it was gone again, and the trees were still. He thought he heard hoofbeats, but he couldn't be sure. The wind, rustling the leaves behind him, washed all other sound away like so much paper on the shore.

Slocum started to run and was halfway to the trees when he saw the ragged brim of a hat, a man on horseback breaking from the wooded clump. The trees screened him almost completely, and Slocum could catch only glimpses. It was like watching someone run behind a picket fence and trying to identify him.

Slocum turned and sprinted back across the creek. He leapt into the saddle and kicked his spurs deep into his mount. This time, there was no doubt about the hoofbeats. They clapped at him just before his own horse broke into a run.

21

Slocum spotted the bunch grass right away. Crushed under the weight of the waiting gunman, it almost perfectly mirrored the lanky Nate Holder... and a dozen other tall, thin men Slocum had seen in the area.

Glittering in the sun, arranged in a neat row, stood a half-dozen or so cartridge casings. They looked like nothing so much as a display of trophies on a shelf. Slocum scooped up the empty shells into his palm and looked at them carefully. They were from a Sharps .50–70 caliber buffalo gun. He wished he knew whether Nate Holder featured the heavy artillery in his arsenal. Looking back, he regretted not finding the casing he'd accidentally kicked into the ravine. He hadn't seen that one clearly enough to tell what it was.

In a spot of damp earth, he found several hoofprints. One of the shoes had a half moon–shaped nick on its leading edge. Three or four prints featured the distinctive mark. Backing away from the trees, he found it again in three or four places in the dry soil. Torn between hot pursuit and a more careful approach, Slocum walked to the front of the stand of trees and trained his glasses on the work crews. He was not nearly as high above them here, and it took him a moment to spot Scarecrow's branding fire. The lanky cowhand was nowhere to be seen. Even Luke Bradley's horse was gone now. Slocum whistled in admiration at Holder's marksmanship. A man on horseback at this range was no easy shot. He felt badly about Luke, but there was no denying that he had fallen under the gun of a master.

Slocum gave the sniper's lair a quick once over. Other than the empty shells and the distinctive shoe print, he found nothing useful. Regaining his horse, he walked the stallion through the pines, then goosed it into a gallop. Reading sign was not his long suit, but the fleeing gunman had made no attempt to disguise his trail. In the occasional grassless spots, hoofprints were clearly discernible. Every so often, he caught a glimpse of the chipped shoe.

Heading up into the foothills, he was only too aware that his quarry had the high ground. Letting your enemy have that tactical advantage was a serious gamble. And when the man could shoot like Nate Holder, it was arguably suicidal. But there was no way to find Mary Alice without taking the risk. At least, he comforted himself, I know he's up there somewhere.

The ground rose steadily, and the grass gradually gave way to rocks. Up on the ridges, tufts of grass stuck up like rooster combs out of the unforgiving soil. Bent by the wind, they were half the height of grass farther down in the valley. But the sudden aridity was a blessing. Nearly every hoofprint was easily visible, and Slocum had no trouble following the trail.

The territory was beginning to look vaguely familiar. He realized he'd been through the area once before, while riding line. He was very close now to the limit of Stuart's land. The next spread belonged to Matt Cutshaw, the fat man who had given him such a hard time at the stock growers' meeting. Slocum wondered whether there was any connection. Had Cutshaw been trying to fatten himself still further, and at Addison Stuart's expense? It was possible, of course, but it seemed too neat a scheme. Besides, if Holder or the rustlers, or both, had been working for Cutshaw all along, the last thing the fat man would want is to have the connection known. Holder would have instructions to stay as far away from Cutshaw's land as possible.

But the high country was really no-man's-land, no matter who claimed it. Most of the grass worth having was down below. Few cattle ever strayed this far, and there was little reason for anyone to want it, except to broaden his holdings. It made a ranch larger, but added little or nothing to its value.

Nearing the top of the highest ridge yet, Slocum reined in and climbed down. He still wore the glasses around his neck, and crept to the top of the ridge with the binoculars in one hand. Dodging among slabs of broken red rock, he found a niche that offered both cover and a good vantage point. He could look out over the floor of the next valley and all the way to the next ridge, even higher than his own.

Holder had a good start on him, but the hoofprints he'd left behind suggested he was in no hurry. Once he'd left the immediate vicinity of the work crews, he'd slowed his pace. The shoes no longer bit so deeply into the dry ground, and they were spaced closer together. Judging by his trail, Nate Holder didn't have a care in the world.

And if he knew Slocum was on his tail, he'd done nothing to let on. He'd tried none of the usual tricks that might be tried by a man trying to buy time or throw pursuit off altogether. Judging by the trail, he could have been a man out for a Sunday ride in the foothills. If anything, he was almost too casual. Slocum started to wonder whether he was being set up.

Sweeping the valley floor with his glasses, he spotted nothing out of the ordinary. Nothing moved below. The birds seemed calm. There wasn't a sound to suggest fright. And there was not the deathly silence that usually indicated the presence of some hidden danger. Far ahead, almost to the ridge line across the valley, a black spot caught his eye. Bringing the glasses to bear on it, he was able to pick out a horseman, angling up a switchback at a careful, almost leisurely pace.

The man's face was averted, and at that range he might not have been able to tell for sure even if he had been able to see the features. The clothing, as nearly as he could remember, was that of the man who'd fled the stand of jack pines. But then, neither Holder nor anyone else he'd see in Wyoming was that distinctive a dresser. One man's clothes looked much like those of another.

Nate Holder had been anything but flamboyant, preferring plain speech and ordinary dress. His face alone was all the evidence anyone needed that this was no common man. So, as the horseman neared the top of the ridge, Slocum knew only that it could have been Holder. Precious little it was.

Climbing back into the saddle, he pushed his horse down the slope, slowing only at the hairpins on the trail as it zigzagged down the rocky face. It was treacherous footing, and a fall could be fatal. Slocum clenched his teeth and breathed through his nose in his anxiety until, halfway down, the trail became a brown streak in gray-green grass. The footing was still anything but secure, but a good horse was unlikely to have trouble in good weather.

As they neared the bottom, the horse seemed to sense Slocum's urgency and pulled on the reins, letting the rider know he wanted to have his head. The horse broke into a trot on the last switchback, and when they reached the floor, he was running flat out. Slocum tugged him toward the meandering brook, flanked by small trees and a thick brush. A cut, probably an old Indian travois trail, was gouged in the earth and the sparse vegetation left plenty of space for the telltale shoe prints.

The trail led to a cut in the trees, and Slocum urged the horse into the stream without dismounting. Halfway across, he let up for a moment while the horse drank eagerly, then shook its mane and continued across without urging from him.

The travois trail angled to the left, and Slocum kicked the horse into a gallop. Flatlands were the only places he could close the gap. Pushing the horse too hard on the treacherous ridges was foolish and needlessly risky. As long as he kept a steady pace on the grades, he could sit on Holder's tail for days. But he knew there was no need. The gunman would not have gone much farther than the next valley. He needed to be within easy range of his principal target, and just far enough away to make accidental discovery unlikely.

Up toward the top of the ridge, Slocum thought he saw a glint of light, something that shouldn't be there if Holder had continued on at his earlier pace. He slowed and watched the spot, hoping for another look. Sitting on horseback it was difficult to focus on a single spot, but Slocum knew the general location, and he kept his eyes peeled. After a few minutes, and no recurrence, he relaxed a little.

The switchbacks were tedious, and Slocum fought the desire to take them at a faster pace. The closer he came to the ridge, the harder it was to keep a tight rein on his own emotions. For days, the Clearwater basin had been a tinderbox. Any stray spark could set it ablaze. For all he knew, that spark had already been struck. Luke Bradley had been popular with his outfit. The men in Stuart's employ were not likely to take his murder lightly. If Clay Hardin continued to fan the hatred, it was more than possible that Linc Brewster and his allies would have their hands full.

But all of that was just so much background for Slocum. The real threat, not just to life and limb, but to the fragile peace of the basin, lay above him somewhere, in the person of Nate Holder. Making his living by exploiting just such passionate antagonism, the man was a fuse in a keg of powder. That he happened to have a hostage only complicated matters.

Finally, the last leg of the trail approached the crest of the ridge. Looking back and down to the valley floor, Slocum wondered whether anyone was following him. He had been surprised that no one had bothered to chase after the gunman. It was possible, of course, that they didn't know where he'd been hiding. Possible . . . but not likely. So where the hell were they?

Slowing a bit to watch the trail across the valley, he saw nothing out of the ordinary. It looked like he was on his own.

Breaking over the ridge, he spotted a line shack almost immediately. Down on the valley floor, hard against a steep rock face to protect it from the winter weather, it looked small and insignificant. It couldn't be Stuart's, because the Scotsman had none. As near as he could remember, this was Cutshaw's land.

Still in the saddle, he held the horse steady with one hand and trained the glasses on the shack with the other. Adjusting the focus, he zeroed in on the ramshackle building. A small railed corral sat to its left, and three horses milled nervously, as if they'd just been disturbed by something. A pair of saddles hung on a peg bar beside the front door. Sunlight, beginning to redden now, glinted off the dirty glass of a pair of windows. Getting down to the shack would be easy. Getting there without being seen would not.

As he started down, he saw a small curl of smoke puff up out of the chimney. Apparently, someone had just arrived and started a fire. Not for heat, the air was too warm for that, it must be a cook fire. Holder must be hungry after a hard day's work, Slocum thought. And maybe, just maybe, a little careless. He ignored the trail, striking out through broken rock and scattered clumps of grass toward the eastern end of the valley. For a moment, he considered going back and riding around the ridge he'd just crossed to come in on the valley floor, but it would take too much time. He wanted to check things out in the last hour or so of daylight before making a move.

The horse stumbled once, and Slocum swung his feet out of the stirrups to protect his legs. The horse lay still for a moment, then got unsteadily to its feet. Slowing his descent still more, he let the big stallion pick its own way through the rocky litter and the slippery soil. When they finally reached bottom, Slocum let out a long sigh. It seemed like he'd been holding his breath forever. His lungs burned and he felt a little light-headed.

Unnerved by the fall, he realized his hands were trembling. He wished he had a drink to steady them. But it would have to wait. From the east end of the valley, it was almost a mile to the line shack. Slocum looked for a place to leave the horse, finally settling on a clump of elders around a green water hole. He tethered the horse to one of the trees and jerked the Winchester free, then opened the saddlebags for a box of ammunition.

Spinning the cylinder on his Colt Navy, he made sure every chamber was full, holstered the pistol, and started for the line shack. Picking his way carefully, it took him almost an hour to get within clear sight of the unpainted wooden shack. He was facing the eastern wall of the ramshackle building. It was unbroken by a window and offered him a convenient blind spot for his approach.

His hand slippery on the stock of the Winchester, Slocum ducked from bush to bush, shrub to shrub. The chimney had stopped smoking, and the place looked deserted. Only a hundred yards away, he thought he could hit it with a rock if he tried.

Licking his dry lips, he dropped to a crouch and started forward. Trying to muffle his steps, he moved slowly, keeping his eyes glued to the front door. He reached the wall after an eternity and sighed when his fingers brushed the rough wood. Checking the back, he found a window, but no door.

The valley was beginning to fill with purple shadows as the sun started to sink. The single rear window was bloodred in the dying light. He took off his hat and leaned against the back wall right alongside the window. Inside, a single lamp burned dully. It was hard to see clearly, between the dirt and the bloody glass, but he spotted Holder sitting with his back to the window. The gunman kept ducking his head, and Slocum figured Holder must be eating.

Tiptoeing back to the side, he moved to the front corner. His Winchester cocked, he ducked under one of the front windows and stood for a moment in front of the door. Taking a deep breath, he planted one foot solidly in the center, and the door flew open.

22

Holder fell backward out of his chair. Slocum fired once, the slug tearing into the table and sending the tin plate into the wall behind it.

Dropping to his stomach, Slocum cranked another round into the chamber. Holder tried to scramble to his feet, but Slocum stopped him with a shout. "Hold it right there, Holder."

"Slocum, what the hell . . . ?"

"Where is she?"

"Where is who?"

"Mary Alice Stuart."

"How the hell should I know?"

"You kidnapped her. Now I'm going to count to five. If you so much as move a muscle, I'm going to blow your brains out, understand?"

"You're wrong, Slocum, I . . ."

"Understand?"

"Yeah, yeah, I understand." Holder seemed genuinely confused. He kept his hands high as Slocum started to count.

"One..."

"Two..."

"Wait a minute, Slocum. I swear to you, I don't know what you're talking about."

"Three..."

"Stop a minute, for Christ's sake, will you?"

"Four..."

Holder shook his head from side to side. The fear in his eyes was gone, as if he'd made up his mind to die if he had to. The bottomless blackness was back, the lips thin and expressionless. He moved so quickly, Slocum almost didn't see it. He fired at the last split second, just as Holder's gun cleared the holster and started up.

Holder had begun to roll to one side, and the shot just grazed him high on the shoulder. Instinctively, he dropped the gun to grab the wound. Slocum crawled forward, using the Winchester to overturn the table and getting to his feet in the same motion.

"Get up, damn you," he snapped.

Holder just laughed. "You might as well go ahead and kill me," he said. "No way I can tell you what you want to know."

"I said get up!"

Holder nodded, rolling onto his knees and standing up like a jackknife opening. The ghostly pallor was even whiter now. He grinned lopsidedly. "Look, Slocum, why don't you tell me what's going on?"

"You know damn well what's going on, Holder. You're at the center of it all."

"The hell I am. I'm a hired hand, I got a job to do, and that's that. That don't include kidnapping no girls. Job's tough enough without excess baggage. Look around. You see any girl? You even see a sign there's been a girl here in the last five years?"

"You got two saddles outside."

"One's mine. The other one was here when I got here. I don't know whose it is."

THE WYOMING CATTLE WAR 155

"Where's your Sharps?"

"My what?"

"Your buffalo gun..."

Holder laughed again. "Boy, oh, boy, Slocum. If I didn't know better, I'd think maybe you been eating some Navajo mushrooms. Where the hell you get all these harebrained ideas?"

"I'm running out of patience, Holder."

"That don't change things at all, Slocum. I can't tell you what I don't know."

"You trying to tell me you don't own a Sharps .50-70 caliber?"

"What the hell would I do with it? I'm not a bushwhacker, Slocum. I'm a hired gun, true enough, but the gun is right there on the floor, courtesy of Mr. Colt. It's the only thing I know how to use. It's the only kind I own. I got three of 'em, but they're all the same."

"But I saw you this morning. Shot Luke Bradley out of the saddle at over a thousand yards."

"Who's Luke Bradley?"

"What about the horses?"

"What about them?"

"You have three out there in the corral."

"Since when is that a crime? I do a lot of riding in my line of work. Sometimes I need a fresh mount. So what?"

"What were you doing over by Stuart's work crews today?"

"I wasn't. Slocum, how can I convince you?"

Slocum sighed. Holder was right. He had no proof, and he was asking Holder to disprove something. It wasn't possible and it wasn't even fair.

Holder, sensing that Slocum was beginning to relent, raised his hands for a moment. "Look, man, I got to bandage this wound. I got a knife on my belt. I'm going to get it and cut the sleeve. Now don't get excited and blow my head off. Alright?"

"Where's the knife?"

Holder turned his back, keeping his hands high. "Right there, on my belt."

"You stay just like that. I'll get the knife." Slocum moved close enough to press the muzzle of the Winchester at the base of Holder's spine. "Don't even think about moving, Holder. I'll squeeze the trigger before you get halfway turned around."

"Take it easy, would you. Jesus, you ought to be in some other line of work, Slocum. Your nerves are shot. And they ain't helping mine none, neither."

Slocum reached for the knife, undoing the leather strap that held it in its sheath and jerking the blade free with a flick of his wrist.

"Alright, put your hands behind your head."

Holder did as he was told and Slocum, hefting the knife, moved in close. He let the Winchester balance across a corner of the upturned table, then turned Holder so his back was to the rifle. Quickly, he cut away the sleeve of the shirt, then backed away. Shifting the knife to his left hand, he retrieved the Winchester.

"Alright," he said, "it's loose."

"Can I put my hands down, now?"

"Slow..."

Holder nodded. He tugged the sleeve free and turned to face Slocum. The wound was an ugly crease, almost half the diameter of the Winchester slug, plowed through the fleshly part of the upper arm. It bled a lot, but wasn't serious.

Holder took the sleeve and bound it around his arm, knotting the cloth with his teeth and his free hand. "Smarts a might," he said, his thin lips relaxing for a split second.

"Where were you this afternoon?"

"Right here. I was up most of last night, that's when I have to do most of my work, you know? I came in just after sunup and slept until about an hour ago."

"Can you prove that?"

"No, of course not. Can you prove I didn't?" When Slocum didn't answer, Holder pressed his advantage.

"See, Slocum, I think what we have is a Mexican standoff. That's what I think."

"I'm not interested in what you think."

"You should be, friend."

"Why's that?"

"Because I think I know what's going on around here. Better'n you do."

"Suppose you tell me all about it?"

"Can I sit down? I'm getting a little light-headed."

"Easy," Slocum said, nodding.

Holder righted his chair and lowered himself into it with exaggerated caution. "To begin with, I think I know what's been happening to them cattle everybody's arguing about."

"What might that be?"

"Well, Brewster told me about them beeves you found in some ravine. I started thinking about it, and I remembered something like it, down in Texas. Man I did a job of work for had a similar problem. Run a big herd in Palo Duro Canyon, and he started losing steers left and right, about the second or third year. I looked into it, and I found out a bunch of boys was hanging out there. Like fringe on a buckskin shirt, they looked like they belonged, but they didn't have nothing to do. They didn't have no outfit, either. None except their own. All except for one bastard. He played both ends against the middle. He run the whole, entire thing. Being on the inside, he knew everything he needed to know. He passed the information along to his rustling pals."

"What was his name?"

"That don't matter. He's dead, anyhow. The thing is, it looks like the same thing is going on here. What makes it different, though, is that only one herd is getting hit. Man was smart, he'd hit ever'body equal. Harder to miss two hundred head than a thousand or fifteen hundred, for one thing. Second thing is he wouldn't have one man mad as hell. Share the trouble, you know what I mean? People in the same boat, they don't start looking funny at one another."

"And you think that's what's going on here?"

"Sure do. Can't prove it, though."

"So what are you planning on doing?"

"Look, Brewster paid me. He don't want killing, I'll try to accommodate him. But it ain't always up to me. He wants his name cleared, and he wants all them nesters and what not off the hook. I can do that, I will. I can't, well, least I tried and took the man's money fair and square."

"You expect me to believe that?"

"It's the truth."

"Convince me."

"You asked me did I have a buffalo gun. I said no, and I meant it. But I know why you're thinkin' that way. I was poking around in that canyon, where them steers was hid, and I found a couple of Sharps casings. Two up top and a couple down on the floor. Somebody up there had an easy time of it, you ask me. Must have been when they killed what's his name."

"Holt," Slocum said, "Larry Holt."

"Friend of yours?"

"Sort of."

"I'm sorry. But I think that's how it was. I think you find that Sharps, you got your man. Maybe talk to Stuart, or one of his hands, the foreman, Hardin. He might know."

Slocum nodded. "I just might do that."

"What do you plan to do with me?"

"You got any objections about telling all this to Sheriff Kandel?"

"Me and lawmen don't exactly get along, if you know what I mean."

Slocum nodded. He walked toward the window and looked out into the deep gray twilight. He set Holder's knife down on the sill, but it slipped off and fell to the floor. As he bent to retrieve it, something prickly showered down over his neck. He reached up a palm to brush at it, and a dozen sharp pains shot through his neck and hand.

It wasn't until he heard the thunderous report that he turned toward Holder. The shot had probably been meant for him. Taking out the window, it had slammed through Holder, leaving him limp in the chair, a black hole just below his hairline. Looking at the back wall, Slocum felt sick to his stomach.

Nate Holder was dead.

Someone had smeared his brains all over the wall.

With a buffalo gun.

23

Slocum pressed himself into the floor. The lamp was across the one-room shack, sitting on a table, but he couldn't get to it without passing in front of the open doorway. Wheels turned in his head for an eternity before he made his move. He fired once, shattering the lamp. The coal oil spilled out of the ruins and dripped along the wall and floor. The flame caught slowly, licking up the dry timbers. He had only a few seconds before it would be even brighter in the small shack.

Getting to his feet, he raced to the rear window, dragging the chair out from under Holder's corpse and hurling it at the dirty glass. Another shot ripped through the open doorway and pierced the wall just to his left. He tossed the Winchester through the shattered frame. Diving through the window, he landed on his shoulder, rolled over once and scrambled along the rock face of the cliff fifteen or twenty yards behind the shack.

He crouched down behind some boulders and waited. One wall of the shack was a sheet of flame now, and the roof had begun to burn. Thick gray smoke gushed up through a hole in the roof, and the crackle of the dry wood sounded like Chinese fireworks. Comet trails of sparks flickered as they rose on a column of smoke, then winked out.

Slocum waited nearly ten minutes, but no one approached the burning shack. There was enough moonlight to use the glasses, but he had to get away from the orange glare. Ducking from boulder to boulder, Slocum put another hundred yards between him and the blazing building. The gunman had to have been somewhere across from the front of the shack, almost in a straight line with the window.

Training the glasses on the moonlit slope, he saw nothing but shadows and silver leaves rippling in the cool breeze. Working his way up the slope with the binoculars, he stopped at every clump of brush and every boulder. As he neared the top of the slope, he spotted a dim outline darting in and out among the rocks. Almost at the ridge line, a horse waited impatiently, shaking its mane and pawing at the loose earth.

His own horse was too far away, and Slocum started back toward the shack. He'd have to take Holder's horse, if he could get one of the saddles off the front wall. As he watched, the darting figure reached its mount and booted a big rifle, probably a Sharps, then swung into the saddle. The horse was already moving by the time the rider found the second stirrup with his foot.

Dashing back toward the burning shack, Slocum headed for the front. One corner of the front wall was blazing, and the flames already had begun to lick at the nearer saddle. He yanked the other saddle off a peg and sprinted for the far corner of the corral, where the three horses bucked and kicked, trying to smash the rail fence.

Slocum jumped the fence and tried to calm the biggest, strongest animal, a black stallion with a white blaze. The horse shied away from him, but he grabbed a fistful of mane and managed to get a bridle on the terrified animal.

He swung onto its bare back long enough to get it under control, then nudged it toward the corner, where he jumped down and pulled the top rail free. The unbridled horses jumped the lowered fence and disappeared. Leading the bridled horse over the fence, he snatched at a blanket and got the saddle on it. The horse kept trying to pull away, and he had his hands full.

Booting his Winchester, he mounted the horse and headed for the ridge. The switchbacks slowed him down, and the gunman was far ahead of him. When Slocum reached the crest, he patted the big horse and nosed him downhill, just enough to avoid silhouetting himself against the sky.

There was no sign of the gunman, and Slocum used the glasses, still dangling from his neck. Toward the valley floor, he spotted the shadowy figure of a man on horseback galloping flat out along the creek bed, keeping to the grass and following the meandering line of thick brush along the water's edge.

Slocum nudged his horse and the animal, still frightened, leapt down the trail with an energy born of terror. Halfway down, he urged the animal off the trail and down the steep, grassy flank of the ridge, angling toward the western end of the valley. It wasn't possible to see the fleeing gunman without the binoculars, but he'd have to take the chance.

As the valley bottomed out, the horse settled into a powerful stride. They intersected the streambed a quarter mile from the mouth of the valley, and Slocum cut through the brush, forded the stream, and broke through the undergrowth on the opposite bank. He couldn't see his quarry anyway, and this would at least give him some cover.

The valley was V-shaped at its eastern end, but the west end was a shallow U and cut between two humpbacked ridges. Beyond the mouth of the valley, open grassland stretched for a couple of miles. As he spurted through the mouth, he reined in for a moment, listening.

Far in the distance, at least a mile away, the faint sound of hoofbeats drummed across the open range.

Slocum picked up his pace, sticking to the rider's tail. The fleeing gunman seemed to know where he was going and made no effort to cover his tracks. The trail wound through the open grass, and Slocum could follow the crushed and broken blades with ease. They hit a patch of stony soil, and something caught his eye.

He pulled up and slipped from the saddle. There, plain as day in the dry ground, was the print of the chipped shoe. There was no mistaking the distinctive mark. Nate Holder had been telling the truth. But who was the gunman?

Back in the saddle, he pushed the horse even harder. The moon had reached its peak and was starting to slide down the other side of the sky. In two hours, it would be gone. Slocum felt as if he was running out of time. Using the reins, he lashed the black stallion, and the horse responded without protest.

They were entering unknown territory now, and the advantage was slipping away from him. He would be hampered by the terrain, but there was nothing he could do about it. To let the gunman slip away now might be to lose him altogether. The whole plot was coming unraveled, like an old sweater. Loose ends stuck out in every direction, and the rustlers were forced to snip at them one by one. And every snip weakened the fabric a little more.

The prairie began to slope uphill, gently but noticeably. Beyond, the mountains, their snowcapped peaks glittering even in the pale wash of moonlight, glowed like beacons. And far ahead, he could see the horseman now, little more than a black blob against the silver gray of the sea of grass. But he was there, and he was a lot closer.

The gap was narrowing, and the tide was beginning to turn. Slocum could feel it. A rush of energy surged through him, like a distance runner approaching the last leg of a grueling course. The end was in sight, and there was no way he was going to let it slip away.

Not now. Not after having come so far.

He knew, as surely as he knew his own name, that the gunman was leading him to Mary Alice Stuart. It had to be. As the gunman reached the ridge line, he turned and looked back. His face was just a smear against the shadows. Slocum held his breath, waiting for the rider to rein in and turn the big buffalo gun on him, but there was no cover except the waving grass. Slocum was closing too fast. Slowing now would narrow the gap even farther, and they were already within carbine range. The Sharps was no longer an advantage. At long range, it didn't matter that it was a single shot rifle. But at this range, the rifleman knew he might only get one shot. If he missed, he was in deep water.

Still faster, Slocum pushed Holder's mount. Foam flecked the animal's sides and Slocum leaned forward to cut the drag. The shadow ahead disappeared over the ridge line, and Slocum cut to the right. If the gunman wanted to risk an ambush, Slocum wasn't going to make it any easier for him. Scything through the thick, rich grass, the horse's legs made a hissing sound, like the tide foaming along the bow of a fast-moving boat.

Slocum broke over the ridge and spotted the gunman halfway down the far side. Below him, another shack, as dilapidated as the first, nestled in a stand of trees. The gunman had a half-mile lead on him, and there would be no surprise this time.

Reining in, he sat back in the saddle, letting the horse take a breather. The animal snorted, its sides heaving like the walls of a bellows. Through the glasses, Slocum watched the gunman dismount and tie up. He left his horse saddled and sprinted for the doorway of the shack. A corral, identical to the other, adjoined the shack, confining a half-dozen horses.

Slocum waited expectantly. The door banged open again and a man stepped out in front of the shack. He looked up at Slocum through glasses of his own. The lenses sparkled in the moonlight. He had a decision to make. Checking the corral again, he spotted Mary Alice Stuart's horse. The girl was almost certainly inside. For a moment, he wondered whether he could cut a deal. Let them go in exchange for the girl. It was simple enough. It even made a funny kind of sense.

But even as he considered it, he knew they'd never buy it. There was no reason they should. They had the girl, and they outnumbered him. There had to be three men, maybe more, in the shack. They knew he was there. They held all the cards. All he could offer them was their freedom, something they already had.

But if they thought he was finished, they would soon learn otherwise. Sliding from his horse, he grabbed the Winchester and the box of shells. Tying the horse to the ground, he started downhill, angling across the face of the grassy slope past the right end of the cabin. His only choice was to push them, make them nervous. Push hard enough, and maybe they'd make a mistake.

As he neared the valley floor, two more men, both carrying rifles, joined the one with the binoculars. They held a hurried conference, then the man with the glasses went back inside and came out with a rifle of his own. They spread out and started toward him.

Glancing at the sky, Slocum calculated another half hour of moonlight. The three men vanished in the grass, ducking low to keep out of sight. In order to spot their passage, he'd have to expose himself to their weapons. He dropped to the ground and started off at right angles to their approach. The ground leveled out quickly, and he found himself scurrying through the tall grass like a frightened gopher.

A shot cracked, but the bullet was nowhere near him, and he ignored it. Concentrating on outflanking them, he pushed himself until his knees and shoulders ached. He reached a clump of trees and crawled into some scraggly brush. Getting to his feet, he could see the scarred hillside. Three smears of crushed grass fanned out from a point a few yards in front of the cabin. He couldn't see the men, but the channels lengthened as he watched.

Turning his back on them, he sprinted for the line shack. Like the other one, this one, too, had a rear window. He tried to peer inside, but the moonlight on the dirty glass obscured the dim interior. He dampened a finger and rubbed a small, clean circle in the dirt. Inside, tied to a chair in the corner, Mary Alice Stuart sat with her head slumped to one shoulder. She seemed to be sleeping.

As far as he could tell, she was the only one there. He worked at the window, but it wouldn't budge. Moving right to keep the shack between him and the three men on the hill, he slipped into the corral. The horses grew restless, but he ignored them. At the front of the shack, he slipped between the corral fence rails and darted toward the door.

Ducking inside, Slocum swept the shack with his Winchester, but it was deserted. Mary Alice dozed in her chair, and Slocum knelt to cut the ropes binding her arms and legs with Holder's knife. She shook her head as she tried to wake up, and smiled at Slocum. Then, as if suddenly realizing where she was, her eyes grew big.

Slocum patted her knee. "It's alright," he said. "I'll get you out of here."

Her arm rose slowly, and it took him a moment to understand she was pointing at something behind him. He heard the slap of wood on wood and turned. But he wasn't fast enough.

Clay Hardin, up to his waist in the root cellar, stood there in the middle of the floor. The trapdoor lay open behind him.

"Not this time." Hardin laughed. His pistol was trained on Slocum's back. The Winchester was out of reach, and there wasn't time to draw the Colt.

"End of the line, Slocum."

24

Hardin fired once, the shot slamming into the ceiling timbers. In the confined space, the explosion was deafening.

"Get 'em up, Slocum. Higher."

Slocum turned, his hands in the air, and struggled to his feet. "I should have known," he said. "All that crying about Mary Alice was just so much playacting."

"You bought it, cowboy."

"Yeah, I bought it. But I shouldn't have."

"Too late for that, now, Slocum. You are about to become ancient history."

"Don't, Clay, don't shoot him," Mary Alice shrieked.

"Shut up, girl," Hardin snapped. "You're nobody up here. That high and mighty shit is worthless to you. I'm in charge now."

"You don't have to shoot him," she said, this time softly.

"I don't have to do anything I don't want to do. Not anymore."

"How many head did you get away with?"

Hardin grinned. "None. Yet. Thanks to you. But that'll change."

"Clay, you..."

"I told you to shut up, and I meant it. You don't get nothing out of me batting your eyes like some hussy. I finally learned to see through that garbage."

"I don't..."

"Mary Alice, if you don't hold your water, I'll shoot you, too."

"You don't think you can get away with this, do you, Hardin?" Slocum asked.

"Hell, yes, I can get away with it. And I'm gonna do just that. You know, Slocum, it could have been a whole lot easier, woulda been, if you hadn't come along. I had everything just right. Holt didn't know shit, and Stuart's a clown. Without me and Holt, that place would have been a ghost town two years ago. But he didn't want to be fair about it, didn't want to pay me what I was worth. So, I reckon I'll just have to take it."

"You killed Holt, didn't you?"

"Didn't want to, but he left me no choice. Once you found them beeves, I was looking at two years' worth of work, all gone. He woulda figured it out sooner or later. Larry was too smart for his own good, and too damn honest. If he'd been willing to turn his back on the whole thing, I could have left him alone, but he wasn't like that. So..."

"And Russ Higgins?"

"That wasn't me."

"You set it up, though, didn't you?"

"Hell, you don't have to know everything. This ain't no dime novel, Slocum, where the bad guy confesses everything before he dies. Anyhow, it's you's gonna die, not me."

"You're running scared, Clay. And that's a big mistake. You'll do something stupid, just like you always do."

"Shut up!" He stepped toward Slocum and lashed out

with the pistol, catching him on the left side of the face. The gunsight raked across the flesh, cutting a ragged furrow in the meat of Slocum's cheek.

"Why, Clay? Why did you do it?"

"You ought to know that, Mary Alice. Better than anyone. You thought I wasn't good enough for you. You never did. You thought better of that dirt farmer than you did of me."

"Pat Hennegan?" Slocum asked.

Hardin raised the pistol again. "I told you once to shut up. This is between me and her."

"You killed Pat?" Mary Alice seemed unable to believe it. "But . . . why? He never did anything to you."

"You were sweet on him. That's why."

"That's no reason to . . ."

"Reason enough. You kept right on teasing me, then pushing me away every time I got close. I could have been somebody someday, if you gave me a chance. But you were too busy looking down your nose at me. If I had money, it would have been different."

"No, Clay, it wouldn't."

"Yes it would. That's the only thing you understand."

"Listen to yourself. You're not making any sense. If money mattered, why would I have been interested in Pat Hennegan?"

"Because he owned his own place, that's why. Him and that sister of his. They were bad-mouthing me, running me down. They wanted to use you to get your old man's land."

"But that's crazy!"

"Maybe, but it looks like I got the last laugh. Hennegan's dead, and I'm still breathing. Another week, I'll be sitting up in some hotel in St. Louis, all the women I want running to fetch me things."

"My father will . . ."

"Your father will do nothing. He couldn't pull his own boots on without having that damn Whitcomb do it for him."

"Clay, you alright?" The shout from outside caused

Hardin to jerk his head toward the door. For a second, Slocum considered rushing him, but thought better of it.

Hardin waved the pistol. "Don't be stupid, Slocum." He backed toward the door. "Come on, it's all clear." He stood to the side and waited for his three friends.

The faces were all unfamiliar to Slocum. They looked at him curiously, but without the malice that distorted Hardin's features. "This is him, huh?" one of the men said.

"That's him, Artie. Tie him up."

Artie did as he was told, hustling Slocum into a second chair and coiling a lariat around his chest and arms. He tied the pinioned hands separately, then knelt to secure Slocum's feet to the legs of the chair. "That ought to hold him," he grunted.

"Now the girl. Check them ropes and make sure she's tight."

Artie knelt in front of Mary Alice, redid two knots, and dusted his palms together. "Right as rain," he said.

"Alright, now you watch him close. I'll be back soon as I can. He acts up, don't kill him, just hurt him a little. I'll kill him myself."

"Don't worry about it," Artie said.

"Let's go," Hardin snapped, pushing the other two men back out through the door.

When they rode off, Artie made himself comfortable at a ramshackle wooden table. He spread a deck of cards on the dirty tabletop, did a quick count, then, with one hand, shuffled them with a flourish. "You ever see anything like that?" he asked.

"Not bad," Slocum said. "You a sharp?"

"Hell, man, I lost more money than anybody you know. Never could pack it in when I should have. Always wanted one more hand, you know?"

"Sounds like your friend Hardin."

"Unh unh. Clay knows what he's doing. He don't gamble at all."

"You trust him?"

"Sure, course I do. Why shouldn't I?"

"Well, you're sitting here while he's out making a killing. You think he'll give you your cut?"

"That ain't what he's up to."

"What, then?"

"Got some getting even to do, he says. Some old man. I don't know who, exactly. But he'll be back. We don't make the run until tomorrow." Slocum felt as if he'd been hit with a fist. He glanced at Mary Alice, but she seemed oblivious, as if she had not understood what Artie meant.

Artie got up. He paced the room a little, his hands behind his back. Slocum watched him, watched the thick-knuckled fingers working like a tangle of worms in a tin can. "Damn, it's close in here," Artie said.

He paced some more, then stepped to the door. "I'll be right outside. Don't think about doing nothing dumb." He dragged a chair through the open door and leaned it against the front wall of the line shack. He sat down heavily, just out of Slocum's view. Only the toes of his boots were cut by the lamplight spilling through the open door.

Slocum got Mary Alice's attention without speaking. With his eyes, he directed her to the knife on the floor. Where it lay, neither of them could reach it, but her legs were free. Tilting his head, he coached her to push the knife closer to him. The knife slid soundlessly across the floor, until the toe of her boot could no longer touch it.

Now, all he had to do was get his hands on it. Easier said than done, he thought. He could fall over, dragging the chair with him, but Artie would hear it. He looked behind him. The high-backed chair was only a foot or so from the back wall. He wriggled his legs trying to loosen the ropes a bit, then managed to get his feet alongside the chair legs. Digging his heels in, he tilted backward, until the chair leaned against the wall.

Artie coughed and shifted his feet, and Slocum held his breath. The big man settled down again, and the scrape of a match filled the cabin with the sharp scent of phosphorous. A small blue cloud drifted past the doorway, and Slocum relaxed. Using his heels as a brake, he nudged the chair legs forward a bit, and the chair slid down the wall a few inches. The scrape of wood on wood sounded louder than it was.

Slocum waited a few moments, then slid another few inches lower. After the fourth time, he could feel the floor with his fingertips. Bracing himself, he spread his hands and shook the chair. It slipped free and his full weight mashed his palms into the floor. Slowly, he lowered himself the rest of the way, but he couldn't get his arms completely out of the way. Twisting his body away from the knife, he fell onto his shoulder. The meat of his upper arm muffled the impact.

Groping blindly, he felt for the knife, but it eluded him. He whipsawed his body and bought a few inches. This time, one finger came in contact with the cold steel. Carefully, he pressed on the knife and managed to rotate the blade closer. When his fingers closed over it, he held his breath for a moment, then tried to lift the knife.

Artie had done a decent job with the rope, and he had almost no mobility. Slocum tried to hack at the rope, but could get no leverage at all. Carefully spinning the knife, he stabbed it into the floorboards, then closed his hands over it. With almost agonizing patience, he sawed at the cords. He could feel each strand part, but the coils denied him any leeway. Continuing to hack, he felt one coil slip free, then shook his hands to loosen the others.

His arms had been tied separately, but with the use of his hands, it didn't take long to slice through the thick rope. He was still on his side, reaching for the rope around his feet, when Artie stood up. Slocum saw the cigarette arc through the darkness, then Artie's bulk filled the doorway.

"What the hell are . . ."

Slocum snapped his wrist, and the knife wobbled through the air, finally striking home just below the ribs. Artie staggered backward, clutching at the knife handle. Slocum tried to stand as Artie toppled backward through the door. The big man landed hard on his back, and

Slocum lost his balance. He fell to the floor, and the chair creaked under the impact.

Once more, Slocum hauled himself up. This time, he let himself go on purpose, and the chair started to come apart. The seat came away and the back clattered to the floor as Slocum stood. Still hobbled by the ropes, a chair leg tied to each ankle, he hopped toward the door as Artie started to get up.

Launching himself through the open door, he landed on Artie with his full weight. The knife handle knocked the air from his lungs as the blade stabbed deep into Artie's midsection. The big man gurgled strangely, and a huge bloody bubble formed on his lips. On its spinning surface, Slocum could see the doorway behind him, then the bubble burst, and a bloody drool oozed down Artie's chin.

The big man lay still.

Painfully, Slocum got to his knees, then to his feet, and hopped back inside. He grabbed his pistol, then bent to untie his feet. He kept watching the door, waiting for Artie to come charging in, but when the rope fell away, Artie still lay motionless on the ground.

Slocum ran to the door and jerked the knife free, pausing to wipe the blade on Artie's shirt. The big man moaned once, then closed his eyes. Slocum ran back to cut Mary Alice loose.

When the rope fell away, he dragged her to the door. "Come on," he shouted. "Hardin's going to kill your father."

25

Slocum was conscious of Mary Alice slowly falling behind. She was an accomplished horsewoman, but nothing in her experience had prepared her for a breakneck ride in the middle of the night. It was a good ten or fifteen miles to the Stuart ranch, and Clay Hardin had an hour's head start. Slocum's only hope was that Hardin was overconfident.

He thought about trying to track the foreman, but there was no point. The smart thing, and his only chance, was to get to Addison Stuart before Hardin. He was already a quarter mile ahead of Mary Alice, and pulling away. He felt a twinge of guilt at leaving her behind, but when he thought about the alternative, he brushed it aside.

The direct route would take him back past the branding corral, and with any luck, Scarecrow or some of the other men would be there. He could send one of them back to look for the girl. The others could come along and lend him a hand with Hardin. The sky overhead was almost pitch-black, the stars bright as diamonds, but useless to see by.

The horse seemed game, and Slocum urged it on with a prod of the spurs every now and again. Every time he broke over a ridge, he strained his eyes, hoping against hope to catch a glimpse of Hardin's party. And every time, he was disappointed.

After an hour, he spotted several dying fires on the plains far ahead. Like inquisitive eyes, the orange flames seemed to open and close as the wind alternately fanned them and let them sink back into the ashes. If he remembered right, Scarecrow was at the third camp, still two miles away. As he closed on the fire, stray cattle raised their heads to watch him roar by, then turned back to their aimless milling as if nothing had happened.

When he reached Scarecrow's camp, he skidded to a halt, calling for the lanky cowhand at the top of his lungs. Crow was asleep, coiled in his bedroll like a caterpillar in a cocoon. The big man spun out of the bedroll and climbed awkwardly to his feet.

"Slocum, what the hell's going on?"

"You got to saddle up, Crow. Mary Alice is out there," he said, pointing over his shoulder. "I have to get to the ranch."

The other hands, awakened by the uproar, jumped to their feet. "What's happening?" They all asked the same question, and Slocum was forced to shout to be heard.

"Clay Hardin's behind the rustling," Slocum said. "He killed Larry Holt and Luke Bradley, and he was behind the whole mess."

"You're crazy," Crow said. "Hardin's a jerk, but he's no killer."

"You think so?"

"Hell, man, I worked with him for four years now."

"He doesn't happen to own a buffalo gun, by any chance, does he?"

"Yeah, a big old Sharps, why?"

"What the hell you think killed Luke this afternoon?"

"That wasn't Clay. Couldn't be. He can't shoot worth a damn."

"Tell it to Larry Holt."

"No way. Must have been that regulator them nesters hired, Holder or whatever his name is."

"You mean was..."

"You got him, did you?"

"Not me, Hardin. With a Sharps. And Holder found some .50–70 casings at the ravine where Holt was killed."

"But..."

"Damn it, Crow, I don't have time. You got to get Mary Alice. Hardin's on his way to kill Stuart."

"You're bullshitting me."

Rather than waste any more time, Slocum kicked his horse into a gallop. Crow could believe him or not, but there wasn't time to walk him through the encyclopedia. He could hear shouts behind him as he headed toward the ranch, still four miles away.

The big horse was getting winded, and Slocum felt cruel pushing it so hard, but there was no way around it. He drove it harder and harder as the ranch drew closer. By the time he reached the bottom of the hill, the horse was near dead. It stumbled once or twice, missing a stride and nearly falling.

Up on the hill, the big house sat like a slab of gray stone carved out of the night. Not a single light burned as Slocum dismounted at the end of the long, winding lane leading to the front porch. He sprinted between the split-rail fences, every step jolting his aching bones. He hadn't slept for more than two days, and every breath split his vision in two. Spots of light danced before his eyes, and he had to close them to keep his balance. A wave of nausea followed the dizziness, and he tried to shake it off as he rounded the last turn.

A sheet of flame shot up in front of him, and he thought for a moment he had lost his senses altogether. Then another spurt and a third, and he realized someone was torching the heavy curtains on the first floor. Pounding uphill toward the porch steps, he saw three horses tied to the hitching post. He lost his balance as he raced past, then got to his knees gasping for breath.

Three more windows were full of flame now, and he heard glass breaking as the flames chewed at the frames. Orange and yellow tongues licked through the shattered panes, and in the garish light, Slocum could see streaks of black climbing along the white walls above the windows.

Getting to his feet, his tongue a boot sole in his arid mouth, he raced to the steps, took them two at a time, and crashed through the half-open door.

"Hardin," he shouted. "Hardin?" His own voice mocked him, bouncing back from the bowels of the huge rooms of the first floor. He raced into the big meeting room. The curtains were ashen tatters, but the flames had jumped to the wooden wainscoting and charred the walls above. The window frames already were glowing charcoal.

Rushing back down the hall, for some reason he thought about the black prints his boots must be leaving on the carpet. Dashing into the library, he shouted again, this time alternating Hardin's and Stuart's names. Neither man answered as he started up the stairs.

Outlined against a wall of orange at the head of the stairs, a man in a checkered shirt aimed a carbine at him, working the lever as Slocum drew the Colt Navy. Without thinking, he fired twice and leapt to one side. The carbine barked once, then fell down the stairs, its trigger man rolling head over heels after it.

Slocum sidestepped the tumbling body, then took the remaining stairs two at a time. On the landing, Whitcomb lay on his back, an ugly gash across his left cheek. The old man, dressed in a nightshirt out of Charles Dickens, lay there moaning, one hand clutching an old Derringer. Neither hammer was cocked, and Slocum wondered whether the batman had used the gun or if he'd been attacked before he had a chance.

Slocum had never been on the second floor. He turned

right into a long hall and raced from side to side as he checked one room after another. Every door was ajar, the curtains ablaze in every room. Two bedrooms, both vacant, had been ransacked, and the bedding set on fire. From the smell of it, they had been drenched in coal oil, and the flames already chewed at the walls. The stench of burning wool and horsehair from the mattresses made him gag, and he backed out into the hall, covering his nose and mouth with one forearm.

Reeling from the heat, his lungs aching with the searing air and choking smoke, he started back down the hall to the opposite wing. As he passed the stairs, he looked down and saw the whole stairwell beginning to fill with smoke. Whitcomb, on the landing, would be overcome in a matter of minutes, but he couldn't stop now.

No longer able to shout, his throat raw from the scorching air, he broke through a locked doorway, shooting the lock off and driving his shoulder into the heavy wood. The door flew back, and he saw Stuart's mother cringing at the head of her bed, a blanket pulled up around her neck.

"Get out," he shouted. "You have to get out." The old woman nodded as if she understood, but stayed where she was, as if frozen. Slocum stepped to the bed and shook her roughly by the shoulder. "Get out," he shouted again. "You have to get out or you'll be burned alive."

"Addison?" She asked, "Where's Addison?"

"I don't know. Where's his room?"

She pointed with a bony finger, and Slocum dragged her from the bed and kicked open a window. Unceremoniously, he shoved her out onto the front porch roof, then sprinted for the hallway. He heard a gunshot as he passed through the doorway. Something stung his cheek, but it took him a moment to realize the shot had been aimed at him.

Down the hall, wreathed in smoke, Hardin's remaining ally took aim again with a Peacemaker. Slocum snapped a quick shot, catching the man in the shoulder, and bulled straight toward him. The man tried to raise his gun, but his arm had been broken, and he couldn't get the muzzle up before Slocum drove a shoulder into his midsection. The two men fell to the floor, and Slocum in a blind frenzy lashed at the man again and again with the barrel of his Colt. Then the man stopped struggling, his hands curled over his forehead, their backs ripped and bruised by the repeated blows of the pistol.

Slocum kicked the Peacemaker away and stepped over the semiconscious man. There was only one room left. As he neared the end of the hall, he saw that the door was ajar. He skidded to a halt just short of the open door.

"Hardin," he called. "It's all over, Hardin. Give it up."

The only answer was a crackle of burning wood and, from somewhere far behind and below him, the brittle crescendo of shattering glass. Slocum barreled through the door, his eyes sweeping the room as he dove to the floor and rolled once. Springing to his feet like a cat, he aimed his revolver at Clay Hardin.

Back to the wall, his eyes rolling in his head, the foreman waved at Slocum with an empty hand. His other hand clutched a Winchester. Addison Stuart backed away another step, stopping right in front of an open window.

"Hardin, don't," Slocum shouted. He saw the muscles trembling in Hardin's forearm, then the finger tightened on the trigger and the room exploded. Slocum fired in the same split second, then again. He kept pulling the trigger, but the Colt was empty. Stuart raised one forearm in front of his face, but it was too late. A bright red stain bloomed like a huge rose on the front of his nightshirt, and he stumbled backward, falling through the window and landing on the roof.

Clay Hardin looked at Slocum with a twisted grin. He squeezed the trigger again, but nothing happened. He had forgotten to lever another round into the chamber, and the hammer fell on an empty shell. Slowly, the free hand came up, pulled the hammer back, and Hardin waved the carbine unsteadily. He looked down at the two dark holes in his chest, then tottered a step or two before collapsing. As he slid down the wall, the bloody back of his shirt smeared bright red stripes on the flocked wallpaper.

Outside, he heard a scream.

He rushed to the window, where Mrs. Stuart cradled her son's head in her lap. "Addison, speak to me, boy. Addison . . . Addison . . . Addison?" Her voice changed from scolding to pleading, but no matter how many times she said his name, Addison Stuart wouldn't hear her.

Slocum climbed through the window and dragged Mrs. Stuart away from the window. Smoke billowed from the lower floors, and Slocum waved to several men racing toward the house. They dragged a heavy ladder with them, and two men raised it to the roof while the others hastily formed a bucket brigade.

Slocum draped Mrs. Stuart across his shoulders and climbed halfway down to deliver the old woman over to a pair of cowhands, then started back up.

"Slocum, don't go back in there," one of the men shouted, but Slocum ignored him. He ducked back through the window and groped down the hall, keeping low to avoid the worst of the smoke and superheated air. At the stairwell, he could still see Whitcomb, wreathed in smoke now, and he stumbled down to the landing and grabbed the old man in a bear hug.

Whitcomb mumbled something Slocum didn't catch as he started back up the stairs. Getting the feathery weight of the old batman onto the roof was quickly and easily done. He slung Whitcomb over his shoulders and started down the ladder, bending his neck and holding onto Whitcomb with one hand. As he reached the last rung of the ladder, he lost his balance and tumbled to the ground.

"Slocum, Slocum?" He heard the voice, even dimly recognized it. He rolled onto his back and tried to sit up. Mary Alice fell to her knees in front of him.

"Daddy?" she asked.

He shook his head and passed out.

epilogue

Slocum lay on his back and watched the sun come up. He wanted to turn away. The color was too reminiscent of the raging flames three nights before, but his skin was still cracked and sore from the searing heat. He draped a forearm over his eyes, but the bright red seeped in around it.

"You alright?"

He nodded. "I guess so."

"Can I get you anything?"

"No, thank you."

He felt her hand on his stomach, the strong fingers kneading the flesh, then tugging playfully at a thatch of hair. "You can't stay like this forever, you know."

"I know."

"Mary Alice Stuart was by last night."

Slocum nodded.

"She wanted you to know how much she appreciates what you did."

"I didn't do anything."

"She offered you a job."

"I don't want it."

"I took the liberty of declining for you."

"Thanks."

"She seems to be alright, in case you're interested."

"She's young and strong."

"And very pretty."

"It doesn't matter."

"It matters to me. Especially because it's been too long since..."

"Since what?"

"You know..."

"No, I don't know. Tell me."

He let his hand fall away and looked into those brilliant green eyes. Her hair was tangled, half obscuring her face as she leaned over him. "I don't feel comfortable talking about it," she said.

Slocum smiled.

"What's so funny?"

"Nothing."

She smacked him playfully, then leaned over to kiss him on the forehead. Her breasts brushed against his chest, and he reached out to hold them in his hands.

"You're not up for that," she said.

"Then you're not looking in the right place."

Her hand closed over him like a sheath of flame accepting a burning sword. She didn't move a muscle. He twitched involuntarily, and she laughed. "Don't be too anxious."

"Can't help it."

"You've been through a lot the past few days."

"I'll survive. I always do."

"That attitude can get you killed."

She squeezed him, and he twitched again, this time by design.

"Are you sure?" she asked.

He nodded.

"Alright then..." Raising herself up off the bed, she straddled him, lowering herself until a tighter, hotter sheath swallowed him, so slowly it made him moan. She gripped him with her knees, wriggling her hips and taking him still deeper inside her.

"What happens now," she asked.

"You don't know?"

"I don't mean that."

"What, then."

"I mean tomorrow, the next day, and the day after that."

"Today is all there is," he said.

She started to raise herself up, and he thought she was going to leave.

"John Slocum, you're a damn fool, but I guess I can live with that."

She started slowly.

And it took them a long time.

JAKE LOGAN
TODAY'S HOTTEST ACTION WESTERN!

_SLOCUM AND THE PREACHER'S DAUGHTER #119	0-425-11194-6/$2.95
_SLOCUM AND THE GUNFIGHTER'S RETURN #120	0-425-11265-9/$2.95
_THE RAWHIDE BREED #121	0-425-11314-0/$2.95
_GOLD FEVER #122	0-425-11398-1/$2.95
_DEATH TRAP #123	0-425-11541-0/$2.95
_SLOCUM AND THE TONG WARRIORS #125	0-425-11589-5/$2.95
_SLOCUM AND THE OUTLAW'S TRAIL #126	0-425-11618-2/$2.95
_SLOCUM AND THE PLAINS MASSACRE #128	0-425-11693-X/$2.95
_SLOCUM AND THE IDAHO BREAKOUT #129	0-425-11748-0/$2.95
_STALKER'S MOON #130	0-425-11785-5/$2.95
_MEXICAN SILVER #131	0-42511838-X/$2.95
_SLOCUM'S DEBT #132	0-425-11882-7/$2.95
_SLOCUM AND THE CATTLE WAR #133	0-425-11919-X/$2.95
_COLORADO KILLERS #134	0-425-11971-8/$2.95
_RIDE TO VENGEANCE #135	0-425-12010-4/$2.95
_REVENGE OF THE GUNFIGHTER #136	0-425-12054-6/$2.95
_TEXAS TRAIL DRIVE #137	0-425-12098-8/$2.95
_THE WYOMING CATTLE WAR #138	0-425-12137-2/$2.95
_VENGEANCE ROAD #139	0-425-12174-7/$2.95
_SLOCUM AND THE TOWN TAMER #140	0-425-12221-2/$2.95
_SLOCUM BUSTS OUT (Giant Novel) (Sept. '90)	0-425-12270-0/$3.50

Check book(s). Fill out coupon. Send to:

BERKLEY PUBLISHING GROUP
390 Murray Hill Pkwy., Dept. B
East Rutherford, NJ 07073

NAME_____
ADDRESS_____
CITY_____
STATE_____ ZIP_____

PLEASE ALLOW 6 WEEKS FOR DELIVERY.
PRICES ARE SUBJECT TO CHANGE WITHOUT NOTICE.

POSTAGE AND HANDLING:
$1.00 for one book, 25¢ for each additional. Do not exceed $3.50.

BOOK TOTAL $_____
POSTAGE & HANDLING $_____
APPLICABLE SALES TAX $_____
(CA, NJ, NY, PA)
TOTAL AMOUNT DUE $_____
PAYABLE IN US FUNDS.
(No cash orders accepted.)

202c

A special offer for people who enjoy reading the best Westerns published today. If you enjoyed this book, subscribe now and get...

TWO FREE WESTERNS!
A $5.90 VALUE—NO OBLIGATION

If you enjoyed this book and would like to read more of the very best Westerns being published today, you'll want to subscribe to True Value's Western Home Subscription Service. If you enjoyed the book you just read and want more of the most exciting, adventurous, action packed Westerns, subscribe now.

TWO FREE BOOKS

When you subscribe, we'll send you your first month's shipment of the newest and best 6 Westerns for you to preview. With your first shipment, two of these books will be yours as our introductory gift to you absolutely FREE, regardless of what you decide to do.

Special Subscriber Savings

As a True Value subscriber all regular monthly selections will be billed at the low subscriber price of just $2.45 each. That's at least a savings of $3.00 each month below the publishers price. There is never any shipping, handling or other hidden charges. What's more there is no minimum number of books you must buy, you may return any selection for full credit and you can cancel your subscription at any time. A TRUE VALUE!

Mail the coupon below

To start your subscription and receive 2 FREE WESTERNS, fill out the coupon below and mail it today. We'll send your first shipment which includes 2 FREE BOOKS as soon as we receive it.

Mail To: True Value Home Subscription Services, Inc.
P.O. Box 5235
120 Brighton Road
Clifton, New Jersey 07015-5235

YES! I want to start receiving the very best Westerns being published today. Send me my first shipment of 6 Westerns for me to preview FREE for 10 days. If I decide to keep them, I'll pay for just 4 of the books at the low subscriber price of $2.45 each; a total of $9.80 (a $17.70 value). Then each month I'll receive the 6 newest and best Westerns to preview Free for 10 days. If I'm not satisfied I may return them within 10 days and owe nothing. Otherwise I'll be billed at the special low subscriber rate of $2.45 each; a total of $14.70 (at least a $17.70 value) and save $3.00 off the publishers price. There are never any shipping, handling or other hidden charges. I understand I am under no obligation to purchase any number of books and I can cancel my subscription at any time, no questions asked. In any case the 2 FREE books are mine to keep.

Name _____

Address _____ Apt. # _____

City _____ State _____ Zip _____

Telephone # _____

Signature _____
(if under 18 parent or guardian must sign)

Terms and prices subject to change. Orders subject to acceptance by True Value Home Subscription Services, Inc.